PRISONERS IN THE SNOW

Drawings by Victor Ambrus

Lothrop, Lee
& Shepard Co., Inc.
: : NEW YORK : :

PRISONERS IN THE SNOW

by Arthur Catherall

Aem

CONTENTS

Also by Arthur Catherall:

SICILIAN MYSTERY

LAPLAND OUTLAW

THE STRANGE INTRUDER

YUGOSLAV MYSTERY

PRISONERS IN THE SNOW

1 :: AIRPLANE IN TROUBLE

:: Twelve-year-old Toni Hoffman and his twin sister Trudi stopped for a rest. They had almost finished digging a path through the snow from the door of the farmhouse to the rough road which led down to the valley almost a thousand feet below. It was tiring work, and they were both breathing heavily. In the cold air their breath looked like white steam.

Leaning for a moment on his long-handled spade, Toni said thoughtfully, "Want to know what I'm going to do, Trudi, when I'm grown up and rich? I'm going to buy a big bulldozer. We wouldn't have any trouble then. It would clear the farmyard of snow in no time at all."

Trudi pushed a wisp of hair back under her woolen cap and laughed. "Remember that story we heard on the radio about two English boys who were always wishing it would snow in winter? They had a sled but there was no snow to play in."

"Yes." Toni laughed too. "And they were always talking about making snowmen. If they lived in Austria like us they'd surely get all the snow they wanted. Look at it," and he waved a hand toward the valley below.

Everything was white, except for a thin dark line along the valley. That was the road, swept clear for traffic by the snowplow just a little while before. A foot of snow had fallen during the night.

"The post bus down there looks like a tiny beetle crawling along," Trudi said. "It hardly seems to be moving."

"But you couldn't keep up with it, even on your skis," Toni said, smiling.

"Well, it seems to be going slowly," Trudi insisted.

"That's because we are so high up, silly," Toni said. "I wonder if there will be a letter from Aunt Ana?"

"Of course there will. She never forgets your birthday." Trudi sighed. "I wish we could have gone down to the village with Papa and Mama."

"Oh, well, another week or so and the snow will start to melt," Toni assured her. "Maybe last night's storm was the last big one of the winter. It won't be long now until spring. Look at the sun."

They turned to stare up the snow-covered mountainside. The sun was shining over the white-clad peaks, and for the first time in weeks the sky was brilliant blue. It did seem as if spring was really coming.

Picking up his spade, Toni said, "Back to work, or Grandfather will have something to say when we go in. I wonder if he had to shovel snow when he was a boy. If he . . ."

Toni stopped, for he had heard a faint hum, and it was gradually growing more distinct. Shading their eyes against the sun's glare, he and Trudi searched the blue sky.

Trudi saw the airplane first. "There it is, way over there, moving toward the Guldahorn," she exclaimed. "Do they always paint airplanes red?"

Toni did not reply. The sun was catching the plane wings, making them glitter a deep gold. It reminded him of a summer butterfly.

"I wish we had an airplane," he whispered. "Or better still, a helicopter. They're best because they can rise straight up off the ground. Just think, Trudi, if we had a helicopter, Papa and Mama wouldn't have to go to the village on skis. They could just sit in the helicopter, start the engine, and away they'd go. When I'm rich—"

Trudi interrupted him. "You're always wishing, and talking about what you'll do when you're rich. Suppose you never are?"

Toni turned away from her, a scowl on his face, and Trudi quickly said, "It would be nice to have a helicopter, though. No matter how deep the snow was, we wouldn't have to stay up here all winter, would we?"

"No, we could go down to the village every day," Toni said enthusiastically. "And when they have the dances in the village we'd get there first, and sit in the front row."

"And everybody would be asking us for a ride." Trudi's eyes glistened at the thought. Then something else occurred to her: "But it would mean going to school every day. Perhaps it is better not having a helicopter."

They remained staring up at the airplane in the sky, and dreaming of helicopters and visits to the village during the long winters. They had scarcely left the farm since just before Christmas. Up here on the mountain slopes the snow was always very deep. None of the cattle had been able to go out for weeks. Sometimes no member of the family dared leave the house, for when the gales howled over the mountains the snow swirled in blinding clouds, blotting out everything.

Today, with the sun shining from a cloudless sky, Mr. and Mrs. Hoffman had put on their skis, and with empty rucksacks on their backs, had swirled down the steep slopes to the village. There was no real shortage of food in the farmhouse, but Mrs. Hoffman had been patiently waiting for such a day so that she could visit the grocer's shop, and the post office.

Toni and Trudi would have loved to go with them, but someone had to stay behind with Grandfather Hoffman, who had a stiff leg and could not walk very well. Besides, there was work to do. The snow that had fallen during the night had to be cleared to make a path to the woodpile, and if they shoveled enough away, the cows and their one pony could be led out to stretch their legs.

The cows were always funny when they came out into the snow for the first time. They acted like calves, or like children just out of school. They kicked and pranced and galloped here and there, sometimes charging into the banked-up snow. Often their excited mooing came back across the valley as echoes.

But there would be no exercise for the animals to-day. The hum of the airplane's engine had grown louder, and there were echoes from it as the high peaks threw the sound backward and forward. Suddenly, however, the smooth purring sound was interrupted with a sharp, explosive crack.

Toni and Trudi stared intently upward, their eyes wide with astonishment and alarm. After the cracking noise, the hum of the airplane's engine stopped and it looked as if smoke was coming from the tiny machine. Then Trudi gasped.

"Somebody's fallen out," she cried. "Toni . . . I saw somebody fall out!"

"You couldn't have! Nobody falls out of . . ." Staring hard, Toni suddenly exclaimed, "You're right, Trudi! Something is falling!"

From where they were standing, it was no more than a speck, and if the slopes had not been covered with snow they might not have seen it at all. Living high in the mountains, both Toni and Trudi were accustomed to looking across great distances, and they possessed very good eyesight. Besides, the clear air enabled them to see better than people who lived in cities.

For a few seconds the speck continued to fall, and then quite suddenly it seemed to grow, and changed in color from black to orange and white.

Toni gave a sudden cry. "It's a parachute, Trudi.

The pilot is coming down. I've never seen anything like—"

"Look at the airplane," Trudi interrupted, grabbing her brother's arm. "It's going to hit our mountain!"

For the moment the parachute and the man swinging gently beneath it were forgotten as the two children stared at the plane. Dark smoke was pouring from it, leaving a long trail across the sky. Trudi gripped her brother's arm more tightly, and held her breath as the plane rushed in a steep dive toward the snow-covered slopes which rose above the Hoffman farm.

"What about the pilot?" Trudi whispered. "He'll be killed if—"

"*That's* the pilot . . . coming down by parachute," Toni insisted, and to show that he knew much more about these things than his sister, he added, "Crewmen in airplanes always carry parachutes. There's only one man coming down, so he *must* be the pilot."

"But suppose there was someone else?" Trudi asked anxiously.

"There wouldn't be anyone else," Toni said firmly. "If there had been, the pilot would have made him jump first. They always do. You know that when a ship is sinking, the captain is always the last to leave. Well, it's the same in an airplane—the pilot would make sure anyone else got out before he jumped. It . . . . oh!"

As he finished explaining all this to his sister the airplane dove straight into the snow on the mountainside above the farm.

Trudi tightened her grip on Toni's arm until she was really hurting him, but he didn't care. One moment they could still see the airplane, and the next it vanished completely in the snow.

A few seconds later, however, they heard a far-off explosion and saw a little puff of brown smoke rising from the spot where the airplane had struck the mountainside. For a few moments the smoke remained, like a tiny exclamation mark in the clear air;

then the wind began to blow it away.

"Toni, we must do something," Trudi shouted. "For all we know, there may have been someone else in the airplane. We can't leave them up there! Don't stand there staring!"

Toni frowned as he turned to face his sister. He shrugged and shook his head. "You say, do something! We can't do *anything*, Trudi. You know as well as I do that we can't go up above the farm at this time of the year—especially after new snow has fallen. Hasn't Papa told us over and over again that if anyone went up there he might easily start the snow sliding down?"

"Ye-es," Trudi admitted reluctantly. She had forgotten the danger of snowslides. When snow begins to slide down a very steep mountainside it comes with a terrible rush.

Toni broke into her thoughts anxiously, "I hope that man with the parachute lands near the farm. Even he could start a snowslide; but if he was near the farm, then there wouldn't be much danger. There isn't enough snow to . . ." He stopped and looked up. Again he shaded his eyes against the glare of the sun on the snow, and a frown appeared on his forehead.

"What's the matter?" Trudi asked. Then she, too, frowned. Down at the farm it was very quiet; there was no wind blowing, and no birds were singing. In such quietness even tiny sounds carried a long way. And from far above they could hear a weird *shusssssshing* noise. It was something like the sound made when a hand stroked along a carpet, only louder, and growing louder every moment.

Toni and Trudi continued to look up. There was no doubt that the noise was coming from the snow fields above the farm. Suddenly a sheer rock wall high above them changed color. One moment it was dark gray—actually it was black, but hundreds of icicles hanging down made it look gray. Now the icicle-fringed rock was hidden as snow poured over it like a waterfall.

The snow piled up at the foot of the cliff, then began moving downhill. Now it was an avalanche, the terrible phenomenon of nature that farmers in the mountains of Austria feared more than anything else. As the avalanche slid onward it would gather more and more snow, building it up into a great wave of hundreds and hundreds of tons that would sweep at frightening speed toward the valley below.

Everything in its path would be in danger. Even a small forest of pine or fir trees could not stop it. The trees would be uprooted or snapped off; houses would be demolished, or buried.

There had never been an avalanche on the Hoffman mountain before, but one was forming now. It gathered speed quickly—and directly in its path, with nothing to stop the rush, was the Hoffman farmhouse.

2 :: AVALANCHE

:: "Come on," Toni yelled, turning toward the house, only to stop and grab his sister by the arm when he realized she had not moved. "Come on, we must warn Grandfather!"

"But the pilot," Toni protested. She pointed to the man dangling below the parachute, which was swaying nearer and nearer the snow-covered slope above the farm. "What about him? We can't leave him. He needs help!"

Toni glanced at the orange and white striped parachute, now only a hundred feet or so from the mountainside. It looked as if the pilot would touch the snow about a hundred yards above the farm. Then Toni raised his eyes further up the snow-covered slope, and shivered. Sight of that mighty wall of snow rushing down would have frightened anyone.

"We couldn't get to him," he yelled. "Come on, Trudi!" As he led his sister back to the farm, the roar of the approaching snow increased in volume. It seemed impossible that snow could make so much noise.

After Toni pushed his sister into the house, and yanked the heavy door shut, the silence was startling. The Hoffman farm was built of thick timbers, and was almost a hundred years old. Not until then did Toni realize how sound was shut out when the doors and windows were closed.

He slammed the heavy bar across the door, then hurried to the kitchen where his sister was already waking Grandfather Hoffman. The old man had been dozing by the big stove. Still only half awake he rubbed his eyes and frowned. Breathlessly Trudi told him about the plane crash, the man swinging to earth beneath the parachute, and the wall of snow that was now roaring down toward the farm buildings. She was so excited, however, that the old man could hardly understand what she was saying.

"Start again, start again, Trudi," Grandfather Hoffman pleaded, and as Toni rushed into the room he turned to him and asked, "Toni, what *is* going on?"

"Snow! An avalanche!" Toni blurted out, and the old man jumped up. He had injured a leg when he was much younger, and now used a stick to hobble around the house. However, the word *avalanche* brought him to his feet instantly.

He steadied himself against the pile of logs stacked

near the stove. Here in the high mountains, the family never burned coal, but instead used pine logs cut from their own trees farther down the hill.

"Get all the shutters closed," the old man ordered. "Be as quick as you can. If any of the windows are broken we'll have the house half full of snow before we know it. Come on, children . . . quickly! I'll do the kitchen windows."

Both youngsters were shaking with excitement and fear as they rushed out. Toni ordered his sister to the parlor windows at the front of the house. He intended to take care of the ones at the back, where the snow would strike first. Despite the thick wooden walls, they could now hear the roar of the snow as it hurtled nearer.

Working with frantic haste, Toni flung open the back sitting room windows one by one, reached out and slammed the heavy wooden shutters, then closed the windows again. He had just finished with the last one when the first wave of snow struck the cowshed in the rear. There was a tremendous *whoosh!* and stoutly built as the house was, it seemed to shiver.

A big blue plate which hung in a wire frame over the sitting room door was shaken off its hook by the vibrations. Down it came with a clatter and shattered into a score of pieces on the pinewood floor.

Toni gasped, and grabbed at the nearby table to prevent himself from being thrown off his feet. That plate had been given to his dead grandmother by *her* mother. It was so very old. His own mother would be horrified when she knew that it was smashed beyond repair.

He forgot the plate, though, when the house shivered again as the main wave of snow piled up against the back of the cowshed. *Thud-thud-thud-thud*—it sounded as if someone was beating the back of the house with a giant hammer. The building shuddered again and again.

If Toni could have seen what happened next, he would have been even more frightened. The snow rose above the cowshed and spread on each side like thick white water. It flowed on to surround the old house, filling the veranda which ran around three sides and covering all the ground floor window shutters. Had Grandfather Hoffman not ordered the shutters closed as quickly as he did, the house itself would now be swamped with snow. The weight of it would have smashed in all the glass window panes.

Hearing the snow rush past, Toni hurried back to the kitchen to see what was happening. Trudi was already there, and Grandfather Hoffman was slowly filling his big pipe.

"I have just been telling Trudi that there is nothing to fear," the old man said. "My grandfather built this house, and he built it to last. It is strong enough to stand up against any number of avalanches. And luck-

ily we have plenty of food, and oil for the lamps."

Grandfather seemed so calm that Toni's heart began to thump less rapidly. Trudi did not seem to be afraid, either, and Toni hoped his own face was not white. He had certainly felt frightened when he was alone in the other room.

"Better light another lamp," Grandfather Hoffman said, and it was only then that Toni realized the kitchen was already lit by one lamp. With the shutters drawn, the room would have been very dark without lamplight.

As Toni reached for another lamp Grandfather said, "If it *is* a big snowslide, we had better close the shutters of the bedroom windows too. You can never tell how high snow will pile round a house. It would be funny if we had to leave the house by the attic window, eh?" He chuckled. "If we did, we might have to fit ourselves with long wooden legs, for the snow will be very soft."

Toni and Trudi both laughed at the idea. If Grandfather Hoffman could joke, then there must be no real danger. Their fears were quickly fading, and they were actually beginning to feel quite excited. This was an adventure they would be able to boast about to the other children when they began school again in the spring.

Toni carried the second lamp, burning brightly, to the foot of the stairs, and Trudi followed close on his heels. When they stopped on the landing to look down, the ground floor of the house seemed very dark. A shaft of yellow light streaming into the wide hall from the kitchen made the corners look black indeed. The roar of the snow had lessened and was now more like a rustling than anything else.

When they got into the first bedroom, however, they could see snow flying past. Already it had piled so high it was only just below the windows, and more was hurtling along in great white masses. There was no time to lose, and they hurried from room to room. They had to open each window, then lean out to draw the shutters, then bolt them.

Toni joined Trudi at the last window, and they looked out for a moment, with occasional wisps of snow striking their faces. A cold wind blew along with the snow, and as Toni drew the shutters his expression was grim.

"I suppose we'd better close the attic windows too," Trudi said.

Toni was wiping flakes of melting snow from his face and did not reply immediately.

"That is—if you think we should," Trudi added after a moment. "I don't like going up there. It is so dark and—"

"We've got the lamp, and we'll get a good look down at the village," Toni interrupted. "Come on."

The wooden stairs to the attic were narrow and creaked, but when they opened one of the windows the view down to the valley was worth the extra climb. They were surprised to see that the sun was still shining. In fact everything down there looked quite normal. The avalanche would probably not reach the village.

"Let's have a look at the other side," Toni suggested, and hurried across the attic to the window with a view up the mountain. He sucked in a quick breath when he looked out, and Trudi gave a startled "Oh!"

The world seemed to be nothing but swirling snow. It was rushing down onto the farmhouse like a mountain torrent, and was already piled so high that the cowshed was completely hidden. In fact the snow was within a foot or so of the attic window.

Just in time Toni opened the window, dragged the stout wooden shutters to, and fastened them; then he closed the window. His sister looked at him with wide-eyed amazement. It seemed impossible that so much snow could come down the mountain slope in such a short time. The attic was the highest room in the house, yet the snow was already reaching up to it.

"What was that patch of orange in the snow?"

"Orange?" In his haste to draw the shutters Toni had not glimpsed the momentary flash of color. But Trudi insisted that she had seen a piece of orange-colored cloth, visible only for an instant.

"It lay on the snow, then seemed to be pulled under," she said.

Toni suddenly remembered. "The pilot! His parachute was striped with orange, wasn't it?"

"Yes, it was." Trudi lifted a hand to her mouth in dismay. In the excitement of the past few minutes they had completely forgotten about the man swinging gently down beneath the orange and white parachute—the man whose plane had brought on this avalanche of snow.

As Toni and Trudi stood silently staring at each other, they were both thinking the same thing: the man had been coming down right in the path of the onrushing snow. If Trudi actually had seen something orange-colored, then it seemed certain he had been swallowed up. His parachute had perhaps billowed out as he reached the ground, but then the avalanche had caught him—and it—and dragged them both under.

"Is there anything we can do?" Trudi asked anxiously, and her eyes filled with tears when her brother shook his head.

"What *could* we do?" he asked. "After all . . . we can't even get out of the house, can we? If more snow comes down we'll be . . . locked in. We'll be prisoners, stuck here until the villagers dig us out."

"How long will it be before the villagers come?" Trudi asked, blinking hard to keep the tears from filling her eyes. Then without waiting for Toni to reply she went on, "I wish we could do something for him. He . . ."

"Well, we can't," Toni said rather crossly. He had a funny lump in his throat from thinking about the airman. "If we could help him we would; but we're going to be trapped until Papa and Mama bring help to dig us out. It might be many hours before they get up here. The snow will be very soft, you know—but I'm sure they'll come as soon as they can."

"Do you think they'll be in time to save that man from the airplane?" Trudi asked. "Some people have been buried in snow for days, haven't they—and been alive when they were dug out?"

"Yes, they have," Toni said. "Who knows? He might even get out of the snow before us," he added, trying to sound optimistic. "After all, he came down on new snow, which will be soft. For all we know, he may dig himself out, and . . ." He stopped and looked toward the head of the narrow stairway. "Is that Grandfather calling?"

They moved quietly across to the top of the dark stairs and listened. The lamp made the landing at the foot of the stairs seem as black as ink, for its light did not reach very far.

"It couldn't . . ." Toni began, and stopped again, for their grandfather *was* calling, and he wanted them quickly. There was an urgent ring in the old man's voice as he shouted again and again from the kitchen doorway on the ground floor.

"You hurry down," Trudi urged. "You can go quicker than I can."

"And leave you to fall in the dark?" Toni protested.

Then as Grandfather Hoffman called again, "Toni! *Toni!*" both children answered, "*Coming!*" and began to descend the narrow and steep attic stairs.

Fear that their grandfather was in trouble made them forget for the moment the airman buried in the snow.

3 :: ENGULFED

:: Hans Asche, the pilot of the plane that had crashed, was a wealthy young German businessman who regularly flew from his home city of Munich to Venice, in Italy. The distance was only a little over two hundred miles, and by flying he could reach Venice, settle his business affairs, and be home by evening. He had done it a number of times, flying across Austria in his red-painted plane, and until this day nothing had ever gone wrong.

Hans had been lucky in getting out of his airplane just before the explosion which had so startled Trudi and Toni down at the Hoffman farm. Swinging gently below his parachute, he had seen his burning machine scream down the snow-covered slopes of the mountain, and had been congratulating himself on his lucky escape. Only when he was just a hundred feet or so from the mountainside did he begin to wonder what was happening below. It seemed to him that the whole of the mountainside was sliding down toward the valley.

Then, when he was about eighty feet from the snow-covered ground, he realized what was happening. He was falling into the path of an avalanche. Unless he was very lucky, he would land just ahead of the great mass of snow that was rushing so swiftly down the slope. If he was to escape death he would have to do something quickly. There was no one else to help him. The whole snow-covered mountainside seemed deserted and dead.

Hans jerked hard on the cords of the parachute, hoping to swing himself out of the path of the avalanche; but he was not successful. He was about twenty yards above the snow-covered hillside, and the first wave of the avalanche was less than fifty yards away.

With his legs bent to take the shock of landing he came down, and at once the parachute flopped limply around him. Now he could hear the thunderous hiss of snow. He was no coward, but the sight of that wall of white rushing down on him paralyzed him with fear.

He could not hope to get out of its path, and before he could even strike the quick-release buckle which would have freed him from his parachute harness, the first yard-high wave of snow was upon him. Crouching down, he dug his arms deep into the snow already

covering the mountain. In this way he hoped to stay where he was, and let the avalanche rush over him.

Hans did stay there for a few moments, but then the real avalanche—a wave of snow a dozen feet high—reached him. From then on he didn't even know what was happening. He was dragged along, turned over and over, and it was the parachute which really saved his life.

Covering him like a protecting sheet, the parachute kept the snow out of his mouth and nose during the first few minutes, and thus allowed him to breathe. He was carried along, then dropped on top of the Hoffman cowshed where the snow was already piled six feet deep.

The sloping roof saved him from being swept by

with the rush, and on down into the valley where he would certainly have died under many more feet of snow. He was still too dazed, though, to realize what was happening. A few minutes earlier he had been floating down under his parachute in brilliant sunshine. Now everything was black as the blackest night, and he was held down by a blanket of snow packed tighter and tighter above him as the rush of snow from farther up the mountain continued.

After a few minutes Hans began feebly scraping at the snow in front of his face. Breathing was not easy and he was fighting for his life. As yet he had scarcely begun to feel the bitter cold. Desperately he scraped free a tiny space before his eyes and nose.

He pressed more snow away in front and on each side. Gradually he was beginning to feel less terrified, and hopeful of being able to dig himself out, when the snow below him began to sink. He pushed at it, and felt that any moment he was going to fall into a deep hole. Spreading his arms, he tried to hold himself, afraid of where he would fall.

From below him came a sound—the creak and groan of breaking wood. Not knowing what was happening, and unable to see anything, he braced himself for a fall. The whole mass of snow beneath him seemed to be gradually sinking down.

There was another loud *cree-eee-eeek!* and the snow gave even more. He slid down several feet, his heart thumping wildly. Then he came to rest on a cushion of snow once more. He could still hear wood creaking, and hope sprang to life in him. Perhaps he had fallen on a farm building. If he had, then there was a chance that he would soon be rescued. He shouted, and winced, for in that little hole in the snow his voice sounded like thunder.

The creak and groan of cracking timber beneath him slowly died away. Hans Asche waited, sure that someone in the building would come to see what had happened; but the silence grew greater. The last creak died down, and his hopes began to fade. He remembered that in the Austrian mountains there were many little summer cattle shelters. If he had fallen on one of these, no one would come to look at the place until spring was well on its way and the snow had melted.

Cautiously he began to dig at the snow again. If there was a shelter underneath him, perhaps he could dig down to it. He was now beginning to feel the first icy chill of the snow biting into his whole body. He must get free, or be frozen to death.

Suddenly more snow fell from beneath him and he sank a little lower. But then fresh masses dropped from above, covering his face and making it difficult to breathe. He was about to give up the fight when he suddenly heard cattle lowing. If there were cattle, then there would be people too. He must keep on struggling. Someone would come to attend the cattle, and when they did, they might rescue him.

With the courage of desperation Hans pawed at the snow, scooping it away from his face, trying to dig a small cave in which he could lie and breathe. Now there was something else to encourage him in his fight. Not only could he hear cows, but he could smell them. From some unseen hole in the snow, warm air, heavy with the sweet smell of clean, healthy cows, found its way to him.

His strength was failing, for more snow kept falling about him, and he knew he was slowly losing consciousness; but he still kept on struggling to keep his face clear. Snow, snow, snow! It seemed to be hurled at him from all sides. It got in his mouth, his nostrils, his eyes, and he was again beginning to give up hope when he heard a pony whinny. The shrill sound was accompanied by the crash of hoofs striking woodwork.

Gretl the pony, in a stall below, was frightened by the snow falling down into the cowshed where she lived with the Hoffman cows, and was trying frantically to break her halter rope and get free. The sound of her fight encouraged Hans to continue his own, even though it now seemed hopeless. More snow had come down on him, and he could not breathe. His flailing arms moved more slowly, but just before unconsciousness came, he swept his hand slowly across his mouth and moved the snow away. Though his brain was no longer functioning, he drew in a deep breath. For the moment he had air.

While Hans was putting up such a fight for life, Trudi and Toni were hurrying down the stairs at breakneck speed. They had answered their grandfather's call, wondering for a few moments what was the matter. Now they thought they knew, and were more frightened than ever.

Coming up the stairs, and causing them to wrinkle their noses, was the smell of water on burning wood. In an old wooden building like the Hoffman farmhouse, fire was the most terrible thing that could happen. No fire brigade could ever get up the mountainside, even when there was no snow.

Since the house was always kept so warm and dry, the woodwork would burn with tremendous fury if it caught fire, and both children were terrified at the smell. Grandfather Hoffman was obviously fighting the fire, but if the flames had got a real hold, the house would be destroyed in less than an hour.

As they came down the last flight of stairs, Toni bounded down three steps at a time, and saw his grandfather standing at the kitchen door. His big curved pipe was in his right hand, while with his left hand he was gently fanning the air in front of his face. "Have you got it out?" Toni yelled, and wondered why his grandfather knitted his brows in a frown.

"What are you talking about?" the old man asked.

"Coming down the stairs, we smelled water on burning wood," Toni explained. "We were sure something was on fire."

"I called you down because I thought something had happened to the roof," Grandfather said, still frowning. "I was sitting by the stove when I heard something come down the chimney. There was a tremendous hissing in the fire, and when I foolishly opened the fireplace door the room filled with steam and smoke. Snow had come down the chimney and put the fire out. I could only imagine one thing—that the snow had smashed in the roof. And I was worried about you."

"Snow down the stovepipe," Toni muttered.

"The roof *isn't* broken in," Trudi said. "We were up in the attic, closing the shutters."

"Hm." Grandfather chewed at his pipestem for a moment, then asked: "How high was the snow? Could you see from the attic? Surely it can't have risen above the top of the chimney."

Toni exchanged a quick glance with his sister, gave a little shrug, and then said slowly, "It may have. We pulled the attic windows shut because the snow was piling so high. It was up to the window ledge then."

"And it was just whistling down," Trudi added. "Masses and masses! You never saw anything like it. Just as if a giant was sweeping it down with a great broom."

"Well, well, well," Grandfather Hoffman murmured, looking at the stove. "You know this happened to me once before. Not in an avalanche, but during the heaviest snowfall ever. Anyway, we'd better clean out the stove and get the fire started again."

It was a six-foot-high stove, covered with green tiles, and the smoke was taken away in an iron pipe through the ceiling. During the long dark evenings of winter, when the snow was falling, or the wind howled on the mountainside, the whole family sat around it.

Mama Hoffman knitted brightly colored sweaters and caps which she sold during the summer to vacationers who visited the valley. Papa Hoffman carved things with his knife—splendid little bears and deer, sometimes old-fashioned pipes—which also went to the little village shop for the tourist trade.

Grandfather Hoffman usually sat and smoked his pipe, telling tales to Toni and Trudi. He was never short of stories and they never tired of listening. The stove fire door would glow pink in the lamplight, and clothing which had been wet during the day would be hung around the top of the stove where it very quickly dried.

But today there were no tales. Trudi broke the silence with a worried question.

"What will we do if the house really is buried by snow?"

"Stay here. We'll feed the cows and Gretl, feed ourselves, milk the cows, and wait," Grandfather said. His eyes brightened and he added, "What do the fir trees do in winter? Many of them are completely covered for months, but when spring comes, there they are—and they look no worse, do they?"

"No," Trudi admitted doubtfully, "but they . . . they're just trees."

"Well, what we'll do now," he promptly replied, "is relight the fire. Trudi, since you want to grow up to be a good housewife, what would Mama do if she were here?"

"Light the fire again," Toni said quickly.

"Wrong, Toni, wrong," his grandfather said, winking at Trudi, "and your sister knows you are wrong. Come on, Trudi, what would Mama do first?" The old man knew the children were worried about being buried in the snow, and he was trying to make them think of other things. Trudi gave the right answer: First the wet ashes would have to be taken away.

"Absolutely right," her grandfather chuckled. "So we'll get some newspapers on the floor. Wet ashes can make a terrible mess, and I, for one, don't want Mama coming back to find we haven't kept her kitchen floor clean. Toni, you had better take one or two billets of wood into the workshed and chop them into thinner pieces. We'll need a quick, hot fire to begin with, to melt any snow that may still be in the chimney."

He was like a general commanding a little army,
but his orders made both children forget their wor-
ries. Trudi laid some old newspapers in front of the
stove and brought a stiff brush to remove the wet
ashes and part-burned billets of firewood. Toni
picked up several pieces of pine and carried them
away to be chopped into thinner pieces.

He hurried down the hall and on through to the
workshed, which was connected to the house. After
putting his firewood on the big bench, he picked up
the hand axe. It was then he heard a loud creaking
coming from the cowshed next door.

Toni half turned, the better to hear, but the sound had startled the cows, and their lowing drowned out the other noise. They usually mooed only when they were hungry or at milking, and they had been fed and milked already. Toni laid down the axe, hurried to the cowshed door, and swung it wide open.

For a moment he could see nothing. The windows were small, and now they were completely blacked out by snow, so that no light at all could come in. Toni went back to the workshed for the lamp he had brought with him. The rich warm smell was reassuring as he re-entered the cowshed, but when he held the lamp high his eyes widened.

The cows were tugging at their halters, and Gretl laid back her ears and squealed. Toni could understand their fear, for one quick glance showed him what was happening. The sight left him as frightened as the cows and the pony.

The massive roof beams, which had once been pine trees growing farther down the valley, were bending under the weight of snow. The roof had sagged badly and looked as if it might fall in.

As Toni stood staring, the center beam began to split open in the middle. The screech of the breaking wood could be heard above the frightened lowing of the cows and the kicking and plunging of the startled pony.

Toni gaped while the roof sagged a few more

inches and another of the roof beams split with a shriek of tortured wood. At first he didn't know what to do, for it seemed that the whole roof was likely to fall in at any moment. If that happened, any living thing below would be either killed or badly injured. Thinking of that made Toni decide he must move quickly. The milk they got from the cows provided the family with their livelihood. If the cows died, his father would be ruined.

Rushing across the workshed, he raced down the house hall, shouting for his grandfather. Trudi met him at the kitchen door, her hands dirty from the task of cleaning out wet ashes from the stove grate. Grandfather Hoffman was just behind her.

"The cowshed," Toni shouted, and in the lamplight his face was white. "The roof is falling in! Come on . . . or all the cows will die," and turning, he rushed back the way he had come.

4 :: TO THE RESCUE

:: Trudi would have reached the cowshed yards ahead of her grandfather had he not suddenly grabbed at her arm as she darted away.

"Get my stick," he ordered, "and the other lamp. I'll be going on."

Trudi bit her lip in vexation. She desperately wanted to get to the cowshed, not only because the cows were in danger, but because of Gretl. Trudi insisted that Gretl belonged to her, and in fact she rode the pony more than anyone else.

The old man was at the door leading into the workshed when Trudi reached him with his stick and the lamp.

"Don't rush," he ordered as she offered them to him. "You carry the lamp and show me some light on the steps."

Trudi had to bite her lip to hold back her anger. She guessed why her grandfather was doing this—because she was a girl. Toni could go ahead and do what he liked, but Grandfather Hoffman thought she could not do the things her brother did.

They could hear the cows and Gretl. The pony was whinnying now, and making a terrible clatter in her stall as she struggled to get free. The warm smell of cattle met them at the door. Toni was standing at the foot of the three steps, his lamp held high. By its light they could see the reason for his excitement and the anxious mooing of the cows.

Where the beam had broken there was a hole in the ceiling, and through this a quantity of snow had fallen. With the snow had come a score or so of the wooden shingles which covered the roof. They were like slates, only made from split wood. Now they pattered down on the snow like coconut shavings on top of an iced cake. The mass lay in a heap on the floor, and the warmth of the cowshed was already melting the snow. Water also dripped through the hole, for the warm air was rising and melting snow above.

Toni and his sister waited a moment, then looked anxiously at their grandfather. He stroked his big gray mustache as he always did when he was thinking hard. The two children watched intently to see if he smiled. That always meant he had thought of something.

Finally he did smile, and then he turned to Trudi and said, "You go back and light the fire under the stove. If there are more than two of us here we'll get in each other's way. And be careful you don't let any of the wet ashes get on the floor boards. If the polish is gone, Mama will notice it when she gets home, and we'll all be in trouble."

He laughed and patted Trudi on the shoulder. For a moment she hesitated. She knew she was being sent out of the way, but she couldn't disobey Grandfather Hoffman, so she turned and went slowly up the three steps leading out of the cowshed.

There was no smile on the old man's face when he turned to Toni. He looked over his shoulder for a moment, just to be sure Trudi had gone, then said, "I don't like this at all, Toni. Those cracked beams are dangerous. If they break, there won't be anything in this cowshed but snow, broken roofing, and dead cows."

"Well?" Toni's heart was beating quickly. He thought he knew what his grandfather was going to say, and he was scared.

"If we lose the cows," Grandfather Hoffman said pointedly, "we lose our bread and butter. Without cows there will be no milk to send down to the valley. If we don't send milk, there will be no money for flour and sugar, coffee, clothes. So . . . we'll have to get the cows into the house."

"Into the house?" Toni was aghast at the idea. "Mama won't like that. Can't we put them in the workshed?"

"No. If the cowshed roof breaks, the workshed roof will come down too. It's either into the house . . . or leave them here; and if they stay here, they'll die. That roof is going to fall."

"Yes," Toni said slowly. "Yes, I see."

"I sent Trudi back to the kitchen because I didn't want her to know the danger. I don't want her to be frightened, but I admit that I am worried. Our house is made of wood; and it was well built. The trouble is that it was built over a hundred years ago. You can see what is happening here in the cowshed, Toni. If this roof falls in, and the workshed roof too, they might bring part of the house down with them. It is only *wood*, and even the best houses don't last forever."

Toni gaped at his grandfather. The idea that their house might fall down seemed incredible to the boy.

"I hope it is strong enough to stand the weight," Grandfather said. "But we must pretend to Trudi there is no danger, and *keep her out of the cowshed*."

"Well, nobody is going to come here once the cows are out, are they?"

For a moment his grandfather did not reply; he rubbed thoughtfully at his chin, then said, "I'm beginning to feel hungry, and I am sure the cows will need hay before the day is out. The hay is in the back part of the cowshed loft, so somebody will have to get that for them, or they'll die."

"But we'll soon be dug out," Toni protested. "The

people in the valley will notice that something has happened, and in any case Mama and Papa will know. They'll all bring spades and . . ."

"Oh, they'll dig us out," Grandfather agreed, "but it might take some time. If snow has come down the chimney it means the house is covered. There will be a lot to dig through before they uncover our front door."

"I hadn't thought of that," Toni murmured.

"Anyway, pretend to Trudi there is nothing to worry about," Grandfather suggested. "We don't want her to worry. You and I are men, and men aren't easily frightened, are they?"

Toni gulped, but managed to nod agreement. He did feel rather scared, but at the same time proud that Grandfather Hoffman thought of him as a man. He drew back his shoulders a little; yet when he looked at the cracked roof beams a shiver of fear went through him. If they broke when someone was in the cowshed. . . .

The trouble was, as his grandfather had just said, even after the cows and the pony had been taken out, someone would have to come back and climb the ladder to the hayloft which covered one half of the cowshed. All the hay was up there, and it would mean creeping under the sagging roof beams.

His grandfather diverted Toni's thoughts from future danger by suggesting that he start bringing the cows out. The sooner they were in the safety and warmth of the house, the better for everybody.

"Bring Lisa first. She gives the most milk," he said, and patted Toni on the shoulder.

Toni set his lamp down at the side of the three steps. The passage between the cow stalls was almost blocked by the snow which had fallen through the roof, and he went for a spade to clear some of it away. Water from the melted snow sprayed about as he threw the first spadeload to one side.

He was digging his spade in a second time when there was a sudden creak and groan above him. He heard a warning yell from his grandfather, and tried to turn too quickly.

His feet slipped on the slush, and down he went. As he was falling, more snow came through the hole in the roof. It fell with little more than a whisper of sound; but it knocked Toni face down into the heap he was trying to move, and covered him with a pile almost a yard high.

Grandfather Hoffman was almost seventy years old, and for a long time he had only been able to walk with the aid of a cane. But in that moment the snow came down with such a rush that the old man forgot his stiff leg. Toni was hidden under a pile of snow and must be got out immediately.

The cowshed was no place for a man who had to help himself along with a walking stick. It was worse

than ever now, for there was slushy snow all over the floor. Grandfather Hoffman took only two stumbling steps, then his stick slid on a wet stone.

With a startled gasp he tried to keep his balance, but his stiff leg got the better of him. He fell with such a thump that his breath was knocked out of him. In spite of that he tried to get up, knowing the danger Toni was in; but his hands slipped on the snow-covered stone paving of the cowshed, and he slid down again. This time as he lurched sideways his head struck the wooden support of one of the cow stalls. It was not a really dangerous blow, but it left him dazed

—unable to help himself, let alone Toni, still lying under the snow.

Curious about what was happening, Trudi appeared at the cowshed door a few moments later. Seeing Grandfather lying by the stall, she flew down the three steps, turned him on his side, and then somehow raised him to a sitting position.

"Toni!" the old man gasped, and he pointed to the heap of snow.

Trudi let out a cry of dismay, left her grandfather, and buried her arms up to the elbows in the snow in an effort to find her brother.

She dragged him out within seconds, and patted him on the back as he coughed and spluttered, trying to clear the snow from his mouth and nose. Grandfather Hoffman pulled himself slowly to his feet, hobbled over to where his stick lay, and then limped back to help Trudi get her brother to his feet.

Up the three steps they went and into the workshed. There they sat Toni on a three-legged milking stool. He was still breathing heavily, and was wet to the waist from his plunge into the heap of melting snow.

"We'll have to leave the cows where they are until he feels better," Grandfather Hoffman said soberly. "He'll need to change his clothes . . ."

"Can't I bring the cows out?" Trudi suggested. "I

take them out often enough in summer, don't I?"

"Ye-es, yes, of course you do," the old man admitted, then briskly added, "But there's no hurry. They'll be—"

"Grandfather," Trudi interrupted. "I didn't go back to the kitchen to light the fire."

"No?" The old man looked puzzled.

"I stayed just behind the workshed door," Trudi confessed, her face flushing a little. "And I heard you talking to Toni. No, let me finish, please, Grandfather. I know it was wrong to stay and listen, but if I hadn't stayed I wouldn't have been able to help Toni, would I? I did pull him out of the snow."

"I was choking so," Toni admitted, "I think you saved my life."

Trudi turned to her grandfather again, her face still flushed. "I heard you tell Toni how dangerous it is, and that I mustn't know. Grandfather . . . I'm not a baby."

"Trudi, you are being impolite to me," the old man said, but there was a little twinkle in his eyes, and his lips were quivering as if he was trying hard not to laugh.

"I'm sorry if I'm being rude," Trudi said, "but if the roof of the cowshed falls in, it will be terrible. The cows will die, Gretl may die. Please, let me bring them out. I *can* do it, Grandfather."

For a moment the old man looked at her, his bushy

eyebrows raised. Then he drew her nearer, and putting a finger under her chin, he lifted her head so that she had to look straight at him.

"Trudi, you are growing more like your mama every day. When she was a little girl down in the valley, she always wanted to do the things the boys did. Anyway, I am sorry you heard what I said to Toni, for I see now that you are not a little girl any more, but a very brave young lady. I am proud of you."

He squeezed her hands between his. "I don't like the thought of you taking a risk in the cowshed, but if we don't get the cows out soon, it may be too late. I will come to the door. Don't walk underneath the hole in the roof because more snow could come down. We needn't shovel any more out of the way—the cows can get through what's there. And one other thing— if you hear me shout, run for the inner wall. That will be the safest place if the roof does fall in."

Trudi nodded, then flung her arms round the old man's neck and gave him a hug, whispering, "I think you are the best grandfather ever."

Grandfather Hoffman returned her hug, then felt for his stick. Turning to Toni, who was still feeling a little sick, he said, "Go and change into some dry clothes, Toni. You'll feel better then. Maybe you should lie down for a few minutes too. A little rest will do you good. I'll keep an eye on Trudi while she gets the cows out."

He patted Toni on the shoulder, then turned toward the door to the cowshed, with Trudi hurrying on ahead. Now the old man's eyes were serious. For the children's sake he was pretending not to be worried, but the danger which lay ahead was very real. If a roof beam broke completely it could bring disaster.

5 :: COWS IN THE PARLOR

:: Only when the first cow was led into the house did Trudi and her grandfather remember that there were strips of carpeting on the floor, and throw rugs too. Of course the rooms were filled with furniture, and many of Mama's best ornaments were standing on the window ledges. A cow could smash all the ornaments in a matter of minutes.

Since the most important task was to clear the cowshed, Trudi did this first, leaving her grandfather to try and keep the cows from wandering about once she got them in the hall. The moment Toni had given himself a good toweling and changed into dry clothes, he started to roll up the carpeting and move the rugs.

The house echoed with the uneasy lowing of the cattle. They did not like strange places, and Grandfather Hoffman was kept busy, his stick banging on the floor as cows tried to get into the kitchen and into the parlor. The well-swept floor boards were soon

dirtied, and when Trudi finally led in the last animal, her pony Gretl, she stood and stared, her eyes round with astonishment and horror.

"What Mama will say when she sees all this I can't imagine," she cried. "These floors will never come clean again, I'm sure."

"They will," her grandfather assured her, laughing. "And I know what Mama will do as soon as she comes in. She'll send you and Toni for buckets, mops, and soap. There won't be any peace until the whole place has been scrubbed clean again. Toni . . . get a hammer and the biggest nails you can find. We must get these silly cows tied up, or they'll be going upstairs to the bedrooms before we know what they're doing."

"They'll need bedding," Toni said, suddenly laughing at a thought which had occurred to him. "Should I bring down the mattresses?"

"What do you think your mama would say to that?" was Grandfather's quick retort. "Go on, get the hammer and nails."

There was pandemonium in the house for the next hour and a half. Big nails were hammered into the planking along the walls of the hall; but there was not enough room there for all the cattle, so two had to be put in the parlor.

Toni looked at his grandfather who nodded and said, "Go and light the stove, Trudi, while Toni takes care of these last two cows. Put on some milk to heat for coffee. Unless something else happens we'll have finished settling the animals in fairly soon. Then I must sit down. I'm sure it is long past midday."

By the time the last cow had been tied to a nail driven in the wall of the parlor, it was an hour past noon. Trudi and Toni were now as hungry as their grandfather, and the cattle were becoming quite restless. In the cowshed they could drink any time they wanted; water flowed whenever they dipped their muzzles into a small trough. But in the hall, and in the parlor, there was naturally neither water nor hay.

"I'll just fetch a bucket or two," Toni said, "then I'll come in for a sandwich and some coffee. I won't be more than a minute." He went through to the workshed where the buckets were kept. Only then did he discover that their water supply had been cut off. He turned the tap and water trickled out for a moment or so, then stopped.

Their water came from a spring up the hillside. Grandfather Hoffman had dug a deep well by the side of the spring, and laid a pipe from it to the house. His work had been so well done that not even in the severest cold did the water supply freeze up—yet there was no water now.

Toni went back to the kitchen, empty bucket in hand and a frown on his face, to report the situation.

"Hm." Grandfather Hoffman scratched at his gray hair for a moment before replying. "I expect the pipe has been damaged where it passes through the cowshed. You'd better take a bucket upstairs, Toni, and see if you can open one of the shutters. If you can manage that, you could pack the bucket with snow. We'll have to melt it. Trudi . . . get the fire roaring away. We'll need a hot stove if we have to melt snow for all the animals."

Toni went upstairs to try to open a bedroom window. The snow would not be so hard packed there as on the ground floor. Even so, he had to push hard to get one of the shutters partly open. Unlike the windows, they opened outward. He scraped snow into a bucket, and carried it downstairs. It was a wearying, slow task, and long before he had given the cows all the water they needed he was called to the kitchen for coffee and sandwiches.

"In a way," Grandfather Hoffman said, speaking through a mouthful of bread and homemade cheese, "this is like being on a desert island. There's nobody here to help us—just ourselves. I remember as a boy, wanting to live on a desert island after reading *Robinson Crusoe.*"

Both Trudi and Toni knew the story of Robinson Crusoe, and it was quite exciting to compare his predicament with their own. Their house was like an island now; but instead of being surrounded by the sea, they were enclosed in deep, deep snow.

The stove was roaring splendidly, although it had smoked badly until all the snow in the chimney had melted. Now, with its iron door glowing pink, and the room cozily warm, there did not seem much to worry about. Only when they had finished their mid-afternoon meal, and were preparing to melt more snow for the cows that had not yet had a drink, did another problem arise.

Grandfather Hoffman brought it up. "I suppose we'll have to get some straw for the cows to lie on, and hay for them to munch," he said. "Can't let them go hungry, can we? If we do they'll be mooing all night and we'll get no sleep."

He struck a match and while he was holding the

light to his pipe he looked quickly at Toni and Trudi.
Neither had spoken, and both were staring at their
empty coffee cups. The old man knew what they
were thinking, and wished more than ever that he
was not crippled by his stiff leg.

Normally, when it was feeding time, Toni, or his
father, and sometimes even Trudi, would climb the
ladder to the cowshed loft. Using a hayfork, they
would send down sufficient fodder to feed all the
animals in the stalls below. Then the only danger was
a slip from the ladder, or a too-wild swing with the
hayfork which might mean a dig in the leg or foot
from one of the sharp prongs. But now the roof was
sagging. Toni even guessed that it might have fallen
in already, but Grandfather shook his head. If that
had happened, they would have felt the house shiver.

"Maybe *I* could climb the ladder," the old man
said when his pipe was lit and he was puffing smoke.
"After all, just because I haven't been up there for
a long time doesn't mean I can't get up."

"You'd fall," Trudi said.

"I don't think so. Why should I? I climbed it often
enough when I was younger," Grandfather said.

"There's no need for you to go," Toni said hastily.
"I'll fetch it."

"Go up carefully," his grandfather warned. "If you
hear the roof timbers creaking, come down at once.
Don't hesitate. If the cows have to go hungry for an-

other day . . . well, they'll just have to put up with it."

He rose and the two children put their cups on the table. All three knew the next half hour was going to be danger-filled; but none mentioned it. They must pretend that everything would be all right. As they walked into the hall the cows turned their heads to stare, and the soft lowing grew louder. Each cow was hungry and needed milking.

"Once we get them munching hay we'd better milk them," Trudi said thoughtfully. "It must be near milking time."

"Perhaps you could start milking them now," her grandfather said.

Trudi gave him a quick glance before shaking her head. If there was any risk to Toni, she wanted to be there. Poor old Grandfather Hoffman was not much use when quick movement was needed. That had been proved when the snow fell on Toni.

He knew she was right and said no more about the milking.

When the three of them entered the cowshed their lamps showed quite a difference. With the cows gone the place had grown a lot colder. Snow had stopped melting from the hole in the roof, and a number of thin icicles hung down. The roof did not seem to have sagged any lower, though, and there was no more creaking from the cracked beams.

Grandfather Hoffman told Trudi to close the door

to the house. "If we shut out the noise those cows are making, maybe we can hear whether the beams are still groaning," he explained.

After the door to the house was closed, there was a queer, uncanny silence in the cowshed. Without the usual warm animal smell, the occasional shuffle of hoofs, and the *crunch-crunch-crunch* as the cows chewed their cuds, the place seemed completely deserted—almost dead.

"I'll go up the ladder," Toni said, hoping his voice did not betray the fear which clutched him. "Then you can pass up the hayfork, Trudi."

"Be careful!" Grandfather Hoffman still had his big pipe between his teeth but he was not smoking, and that meant he was worried.

Toni tested the ladder, and winced as a loud creak came from the roof beam against which it rested. He shot a quick glance at his grandfather, and was relieved to see that the old man was now poking into his pipe with a piece of wire he always kept in his pocket for pipe cleaning.

Toni put a foot on the first rung, then his other foot on the second rung. There was another creak, and still Grandfather Hoffman was busy with his pipe. Toni went slowly up the ladder, testing each rung as he went, and waiting for each new creak.

"Have you got the hayfork, Trudi?" he heard his grandfather ask, and the old man did not seem the

least bit worried. Toni wondered if he'd heard the creaking.

The ladder swayed a little as Trudi came forward with the hayfork and stepped onto the bottom rung. Fully testing his courage, Toni climbed further up the ladder and onto the hay platform.

Only when he moved deeper into the hayloft did he realize how much the roof had sagged. Normally he could stand up at the highest point of the slope. Now he had to bend well down.

He sneezed when he dug into the hay, and the sound was like thunder. The pollen from the hay always made him sneeze, but somehow today the sound seemed much louder than usual.

Digging as deep as he could, he heaved a forkful of hay around and sent it rustling down the ladder. His nerves were taut, and he determined to get as much hay with each thrust as he could. Perhaps if he got enough down it would last until they were dug out. He went on eagerly, the hay falling with a steady *Sssssssh! Sssssssssh! Sssssssssssh!*

He was beginning to perspire when Grandfather shouted, "Don't bury us, Tony! We haven't got a thousand cows. I think that will be enough. It all has to be carried into the house, you know. Just stay there a minute or so while we see how much we've got."

Toni wiped his face with the back of his right hand. He was sweating now and breathing heavily. He walked to the edge of the hayloft platform and looked down.

He had not realized how hard he had been working until he saw the pile of hay below. Trudi had been carrying it in great armfuls into the workshed, but even so there was a pile over six feet high.

His grandfather looked up and gave him an encouraging wink. "We'll make a farmer of you yet, Toni" he chuckled. "Anyone who can work as hard as that will be a rich man. Just let Trudi get a few more armfuls out of the way, then you can send a bit more down. With luck I think it will see us through. I'll go and see how much there is."

The old man limped slowly up the three steps to look into the workshed and get a better idea of how much Trudi had carried away.

Toni could hear his grandfather and Trudi talking, and he was turning back to bring more hay nearer the edge of the hayloft platform when a new sound stopped him. It was so unexpected that it sent an icy shiver down his spine, and the short hairs on his neck prickled as if they had suddenly changed into tiny wires. He had a queer feeling that he was not alone in the hayloft. He was sure he had heard a voice.

He stood waiting and listening, every muscle tense. Then it came again, making him stiffen with fear.

"Oooo-oooh!"

The sound was half a sigh, half a groan, and where

it came from Toni had no idea. He looked around, his mouth gone dry and his heart beating wildly.

"*Oooo-aaaah!*"

There was the moan again, and now it seemed to come from behind him. If Toni had not been afraid that the roof might fall in on him at any moment, the sound would not have frightened him so much. As it was, he swung round quickly, sure he would see somebody, and the end of the hayfork caught in one of the roof beams.

Toni staggered and one foot went over the edge of the loft into space.

6 :: ANOTHER PRISONER

:: A moment later Toni was falling, one hand sliding over the rungs of the ladder. He had no time to be frightened, for the next instant he was face down in the six-foot pile of soft, pillow-like hay. Before he could sink into the pile, he rolled gently down its sloping side and onto the cowshed floor.

Grandfather and Trudi were just coming back into the cowshed when he fell, and they stood and stared, too amazed even to cry out. Then, as Toni started to get to his feet, Trudi ran to him, her face white. "Are you hurt? What happened? Are you all right?"

To Grandfather Hoffman it was quite obvious that Toni was not seriously hurt. He had got to his feet without trouble, and his face registered only surprise. There was no frown suggesting he was in pain. Trudi seemed more shocked than her brother, and to take her mind off the accident the old man began to laugh as he asked, "Do you always come down the hay ladder that way, Toni?"

"Don't make fun of him, Grandfather," Trudi said, suddenly angry. "He could easily have killed himself, and . . ."

"With a great pile of hay waiting for him," the old man chuckled. "No, no, Toni's too smart for that. Anyway, what were you doing?"

Toni gulped. His heart was fluttering, but it was only from fright—he was quite unhurt. Shooting a quick glance at his grandfather and then at his sister, he gave a sheepish grin. It would sound too silly if he said he thought he had heard a voice, and that it was this "voice" which had made him turn and lose his balance.

Forcing a little laugh he said, "I . . . don't really know what I was doing. I was turning, and I think I caught the hayfork against something. The next thing—I was down on the hay."

"Well, don't do it again," Grandfather Hoffman urged, winking. "If there hadn't been as big a pile of hay as this waiting for you, you'd have found the floor hard, very hard."

"Mama always says accidents come in threes," Trudi said earnestly. "First the snow fell on you; now you've fallen on the hay. What will the third—?"

"Oh, come on, come on," Grandfather Hoffman coaxed. "Let's not listen to old women's tales. We

have to carry the rest of this hay into the workshed, and take enough into the house to give the cattle a feed. Then I think we'll have earned a rest before the stove. You may feel all right, Toni, but I'm tired."

They carried all the hay from the cowshed, stacked some in the workshed, and distributed enough in front of each cow, and Gretl the pony, to keep them quiet for the next few hours. By then it was milking time and Trudi got her stool and a pail; Toni followed her example. Trudi milked the cows in the parlor while Toni worked in the hall, and Grandfather Hoffman went off to the kitchen.

The cows in the hall munched away, tails swishing from side to side, while Toni kept his forehead against the flank of the first cow and watched the frothy white milk begin to cover the bottom of his pail. For some reason his thoughts suddenly turned back to the few moments on the hayloft platform, just before he fell. In his imagination he could hear once more the faint moan which had so bewildered him. The milk ceased hissing into the pail as he tried to think what could have made the low groaning. Then he gasped as a startling thought occurred to him.

The pilot from the plane which had crashed! Why had he not thought of him before? Trudi had insisted she saw something orange-colored vanish beneath the snow as the avalanche swept down onto the Hoffman farm building. If the man had been caught in his parachute, then he could have been carried on down to the farm—and perhaps been deposited on top of the cowshed.

After standing his little stool and the bucket against the wall, Toni walked slowly toward the kitchen. Grandfather Hoffman had said he would prepare a proper meal while the two children were milking, and an appetizing smell of cooking sausage met Toni as he left the hall.

Grandfather looked up. The sausages were sizzling

merrily and the old man was peeling potatoes. He stopped for a moment with knife and potato in hand, for he could see that Toni was worried.

"When I fell, Grandfather," Toni began, "I didn't tell you the truth. No, I don't mean I told a lie—I did catch the pitchfork against a roof beam . . . but something had frightened me just before that."

He went on to tell of the two peculiar sounds he had heard. Groans . . . as if someone was only half conscious. His grandfather did not interrupt, but when Toni finished, the old man got to his feet. He laid the knife and potato down, then motioned with his right hand toward the door.

They passed the door of the parlor where Trudi was milking away. She was so busy she did not hear them go on to the end of the hall, and through the door leading to the workshed and on into the cowshed.

Grandfather Hoffman turned up the lamp to give them more light; holding it as high as he could, he stared in silence at the sagging roof beams and the hole where the slates had been forced through by the weight of snow. The light was reflected sharply from a score of small icicles, and beyond them there seemed to be a dark cavity extending up into the snow.

"Shout, Toni," the old man said. "Wait a moment, though. We'd better get back into the doorway first.

In the mountains shouting will sometimes disturb delicately balanced stones, so here it might bring down more snow, or even the roof."

They retreated to the doorway leading to the workshed. The doorframe was of stone, two massive slabs with a piece of thick stone over the top. It would need more than a shout to bring those stones tumbling down.

"Now," the old man said, "shout *hello!*"

It seemed odd to shout in such a place as a cowshed, but Toni cupped his hands about his mouth and yelled. "Hello . . ." His voice was shrill, and both he and Grandfather were surprised to hear a sudden tinkle as an icicle snapped off and fell to the ground.

"Hello . . . hello . . . hello . . . hello . . . !"

"All right, Toni. Be quiet for a minute and we'll see if there is any reply," Grandfather urged.

They remained quiet for only a few seconds before they were startled by a sharp voice, "What's the matter?"

The question shocked them both, for they had forgotten Trudi, and had not given a thought to the fact that she would be sure to hear anyone shouting.

"*Sssssh!*" Grandfather cautioned, lifting a finger to his lips. "Come here, and listen."

A minute passed, and no sound disturbed the silence. Toni looked sideways at his grandfather and the old man nodded. Toni cupped his hands, turned his face upward again, and once more yelled "hello" three times.

"What is he shouting for?" Trudi whispered, pulling gently at her grandfather's coat sleeve.

"Well, we think . . ." Grandfather Hoffman began, but he did not finish the explanation. Some snow fell from the darkness of the hole in the roof. It struck the heap of snow below and scattered particles of white, almost like a tiny bomb exploding.

"Call again, but not so loud this time," Grandfather Hoffman ordered. "Your voice might have brought the snow down . . . but maybe it was something else."

"Hello-o-o!"

Two more chunks fell, then an even larger one, followed by something solid. Three pairs of eyes followed the object as it struck the snow which was now hardening as the cold in the cowshed grew more intense.

"It's a watch!" Trudi whispered in awe. "A wrist watch. Grandfather . . . it must be the pilot! I told Toni he was in the snow. I saw his orange para . . ."

"*Sssh . . . ssssh . . . ssssh!*" Grandfather limped slowly down to the cowshed floor; holding the light as high as he could, he called up to the darkness overhead. "If you can hear me, drop another piece of snow—or speak."

There followed a few moments of silence, and then a whisper, so faint they could barely hear the words, came down from the darkness above.

"Help. Help me, please. Help."

Trudi and her brother exchanged quick, startled glances. A man *was* up there—a man who was even more a prisoner of the snow than they were.

Grandfather Hoffman called up again, "Hello, hello, you up there. Keep up your courage. We will be back in a few minutes with some hot coffee. Then we'll figure out how we can rescue you. Can you hear me?"

In the silence which followed they heard the man's weak voice once more, but they couldn't make out what he said.

"Pick up the watch, Toni," Grandfather Hoffman ordered, and then he turned to Trudi. "Go and put some milk on for coffee."

Trudi hesitated. "How . . . how can we give him coffee?" she whispered, keeping her voice low so that the man above would not hear them. "We can't reach him."

Grandfather smiled. "If we tie two or three hay-rakes together, we can make a pole long enough to reach up to him. We'll put the coffee in a bottle." He laid a hand gently on Trudi's head and said, "When a man is in danger, Trudi, we never say 'can't' until we've tried everything, eh?"

Trudi nodded and hurried off to the kitchen.

As Toni and his grandfather walked back into the

house, both were worrying about the same thing. Toni put it into words: "I just can't see how we can get him down, Grandfather. Can you?"

"Not at the moment," the old man agreed. "We know there is a hole in the roof, and we could get the end of a ladder through it—if that roof beam would bear the ladder's weight. Trouble is the roof beam is badly cracked, and there is always the danger, even if somebody got up there, that the moment the beam was disturbed, a great pile of snow would fall down. I—"

"But we *must* get him down," Trudi interrupted. "If we don't, he'll die."

"Yes, I know," Grandfather agreed. "On the other hand . . . if we did put a ladder up through the hole in the roof, and the roof fell in, the man might die, and whoever was trying to rescue him might die too." He paused, and after a moment or so said sadly, "If only I didn't have this stiff leg. Trouble is that all I can do is give advice."

Toni looked sideways at his grandfather, then said soberly, "Well . . . maybe I could do it." His voice sounded quite normal, but his heart was racing madly, and the moment he had spoken he almost wished he had not made the offer.

"It could be very dangerous, Toni," Grandfather Hoffman said. "I don't like it at all. Anyway, first of all we'll give him a drink of hot coffee with some brandy in it. That'll make him feel better, at least."

"And then?" Trudi asked.

"Well . . . maybe it won't be long before people from the village get here and dig us out," Grandfather said.

"How long?" Toni asked.

The old man sighed and shook his head. Suddenly he looked very old and tired. "I don't know how long they will be, Toni. But I do know the snow is at least up to the chimney, so it might take them a day—or even longer."

"By then the man may be dead," Trudi insisted. "Toni . . . we could . . ."

"Yes," Toni said, and now for some reason he did not feel quite as afraid. "We'll have to get him out. We can't leave him there. After all, we are hoping people will dig us out, aren't we? How would we feel if no one came to rescue us? We'll have to try to help him."

Grandfather Hoffman sighed again, but he nodded agreement. "All right. We'll try." It was obvious he was very worried, though. He knew the dangers the children would face, far better than they did. Would he be doing right to allow his grandchildren to risk their lives for a man they did not even know? It was a great responsibility, and he felt so helpless. What use was an old man with a stiff leg? He could only stand and watch! Wearily he sat down and began to fill his pipe.

Suddenly an arm rested across his shoulders, and Trudi's soft cheek brushed against his. "Don't worry, Grandfather," she whispered. "We can do it. I know we can." And she gave him a hug.

Somehow that hug seemed to take a great weight off Grandfather's shoulders.

7 :: FREEING THE PILOT

:: The cows in the hall and the parlor were still munching hay as Toni, Trudi, and Grandfather hurried back out to the cowshed. But the animals were lowing now and then as if to point out that it was already long past the usual milking time.

Trudi and Toni fastened the rakes together before they poured the hot coffee and brandy into the bottle, for Grandfather had reminded them that the drink would help the man most if it was still hot. No time would have to be lost between filling the bottle and getting it to him. They just hoped they could raise it near enough to the trapped pilot for him to take it off the rakes.

Grandfather Hoffman held a lamp as high as he could while the bottle, fastened to the end of the rakes, was pushed upward through the hole. He had already shouted to the man that a drink was coming up to him.

A few pieces of snow came down, for it was not easy to keep the long pole steady.

"Can you see the bottle of coffee?" Grandfather Hoffman bellowed. "It must be quite close to you now. It is looped with string on the end of a hayrake. Just lift it off gently."

There was no reply, or at least they couldn't hear anything. On their way out they had forgotten to close the doors between them and the house, and the lowing of the cows drowned out all other sounds.

Trudi ran back and closed both doors, leaving Toni holding the rakes and the bottle of coffee. It was much quieter in the cowshed after the doors were closed, and Grandfather Hoffman called up a second time; but again there was no reply.

"Perhaps he has fainted," Trudi suggested.

They lowered the coffee, for holding it up made their arms ache. Several more times Grandfather called up, but there was still no reply. Then Toni suggested, "If we put the hayloft ladder against the hole in the roof, I might be able to give him a drink."

All three turned to look up at the hole. Because of the cracked beams the roof had lowered. In the lamplight icicles winked and glistened, and the hole in the snow above the roof looked black and frightening. They could see no sign of life, yet somewhere in the darkness up there a man lay, desperately needing help.

People who knew said that when someone was lost in the snow he grew tired, and gradually did not feel the cold. He drifted off to sleep, and never woke again. That would happen to this man unless they could get him down and into the warmth of the house. Yet if anyone climbed up to him and began digging, snow and roof as well might collapse.

Trudi broke the silence, and helped her brother and grandfather come to a decision. "I keep thinking how awful it would be if it were one of you, or Papa."

Toni looked at his grandfather, and after a moment the old man nodded. They must at least try to rescue the man.

With Trudi and Grandfather helping, Toni took the heavy hay ladder from its place against the loft. As gently as possible he leaned it against the beam underneath the hole. All three held their breath as he let the ladder's weight rest against the beam. For a few moments there was a creaking and groaning from the split pine, but gradually it died away. When Toni put a foot on the bottom rung of the ladder, though, the beam creaked even more. Icicles fell, tinkling like breaking glass as they shattered on the floor.

All three hurried toward the door leading into the workshed; but the creaking stopped again, and nothing happened. Trudi chewed nervously on her lower lip; Grandfather Hoffman scratched behind his ear, a sign that he was either thinking deeply or was very worried.

The creaking of the splintered beam had made Toni nervous. If either his sister or his grandfather had suggested that it was too dangerous to go up the ladder, he would have happily agreed. It certainly did not seem safe. But since no one spoke he walked back to the ladder and this time put both feet on the bottom rung. One more icicle came down, and the roof beam creaked and shook, but nothing more happened.

Then Trudi came over and handed him the bottle of coffee. Toni stuffed it into the pocket of his coat, looked across at his grandfather, then slowly climbed another rung. At once the ladder trembled under his weight as the beam against which it rested groaned and swayed some more.

Trudi went back to her grandfather; sliding her left hand into his big right one, she stood and watched, hardly daring to breathe as Toni went up another rung of the ladder.

He could feel it swaying gently as the weakened beam above gave a little and then sprung back. Twice he stopped as tiny fragments of snow fell past him. He winced each time, half expecting more to follow; but none did.

Higher and higher he went, past the cracked beam, past the roof frame from which so many of the wooden shingles had fallen. Now he was in the black hole left by the snow which had fallen through the gap in the roof to the floor of the cowshed. It was much colder up here, and a shiver ran through him.

In the almost complete darkness he realized that he should have brought a lamp with him. Grandfather was holding the lamp as high as he could, but Toni's body blocked out most of the light.

Steadying himself, he looked about in the darkness but could see nothing. In a rather shaky voice he asked, "Hello, sir, where are you? Can you hear me? Hello! HELLO!" As he raised his voice the sound seemed to thunder back at him like echoes in the hills.

There was a weak groan from Toni's left. He stared into the gloom, his eyes now beginning to grow accustomed to the darkness, and thought he saw something move. Hanging on to the top of the ladder with his right hand, he reached out with his left. He touched something, and found he was gripping a man's fingers. They felt stiff and terribly cold, and there was a layer of snow on them.

"Have you found him?" The voice came up to Toni with a hollow boom, causing him to jump. It was Grandfather Hoffman and he continued before Toni could reply, "Stay where you are. Trudi is getting a pole, and I'll hand the lamp up to you on the end of it."

Still holding on to the man's hand, Toni waited. Then, slowly, the darkness of the snow cavern began to vanish as the lamp was pushed up to him on the end of a pole.

When he took the light and brought it level with his waist, the cavern suddenly turned into a fairyland. The snow changed from black to a dazzling white. Toni was in a hollowed-out cave dotted with millions of shimmering pinpoints of color—red, yellow, blue, green, white, all of them winking and flashing as the lamp swayed in his hand.

At any other time he would have stared in wonder at the beauty of it all. Now he was concerned only with finding a place where he could put his lamp so that he could have both hands free. The bottle of coffee in his pocket was warm against his thigh, reminding him that the man he had come to rescue needed warmth, and needed it as quickly as possible.

He scooped out a niche in the snow and stood the lamp in it. Then he turned to look for the man. Only his head and part of his shoulders were visible. His arms were free, but the rest of his body and his legs were locked in the snow.

Toni had to lean forward to get near enough to touch the man's face, and at the movement the ladder quivered. For a moment Toni hesitated, afraid of what might happen; then the sight of the man's face, powdered with snow, stirred him to take the risk.

It took several minutes to get the man to lift his head, for he was only half conscious. But when Toni finally managed to get the warm mouth of the bottle to the man's lips, he responded immediately. His half-

closed eyes opened, he blinked and then began to
drink. All the while he stared gratefully at Toni.

Several times the man coughed and spluttered, but
the coffee was giving him strength. His right hand
came slowly around and he clasped it over Toni's,
helping hold the bottle in place.

When the bottle was empty, Toni stuffed it into his
pocket, then asked, "How are you feeling now, sir?"

The man slowly lifted his head again, and stared
at Toni. His lips began to move, but for a moment no
sound came. Then he whispered, "God bless you,

boy. I think I was dying when you came. Where am
I? Are you one of a rescue party? Will it be long before they dig me out?"

Toni did not know what to say. He couldn't bear
to tell this man that there was no real rescue party,
and that he and his sister and grandfather were also
prisoners in the snow.

"I'm Toni Hoffman," he replied, "and you are lying
in the snow on top of our cowshed. I have come up
through a hole in the cowshed roof, and we will have
to get you down this way. Can you move?"

For a moment the man lay staring at Toni, then he
shook his head.

"I feel as if I am frozen into a block of ice," he
whispered. "Tell them I'll have to be dug out. I am
Hans Asche. They may be looking for me. I am so
weak I just can't do anything. How long will it be before you get me out? I can't stand much more." Even
as he was speaking, his voice had become weaker,
then it trailed off into silence and his face lowered
into the snow again.

Toni descended the ladder and told his story.
Trudi's eyes filled with tears, but she blinked very
hard to keep from crying. Grandfather Hoffman filled
his pipe, but made no attempt to light the tobacco.
He was thinking.

Finally he said, "If you try to dig him out, Toni . . .
I have a feeling that even if the roof doesn't fall in,

a lot of snow will come down. And when that happens, you and he are likely to fall down too."

"Does that mean we can't help him?" Trudi asked, and there was a quiver in her voice.

Her grandfather did not reply, but scratched behind his right ear again. "I suppose we could bring down a lot of hay," he said. "That would break your fall; but I don't know whether that would be enough. There would be two of you, and . . ."

"I know!" Toni's eyes shone in the lamplight at the idea which had suddenly come to him. "Do you remember when the circus came to the valley last year? There was a man who rode a bicycle across a tightrope. He carried a girl on his shoulders."

"Yes, I remember," Grandfather agreed. "But I don't see what—"

"They had a net stretched underneath them—" Toni began, and was interrupted by Trudi who gave an excited squeal and shouted, "Yes, a safety net. I remember. I couldn't bear to look until Papa said that even if the man fell off, neither he nor the girl would be hurt."

"Well?" For a moment Grandfather Hoffman still failed to see why the children should be so excited. Then he realized what a safety net could do. His eyes lit up. "Yes, of course. We could do that. Now where are the hay nets?"

Up on the mountain slopes the Hoffman haystacks

always had to be protected by nets. These were slung over the stacks, and stones were tied on the bottom of the nets so that even the strongest winds wouldn't be able to tear them away. The netting held the hay down until it was time to bring it into the loft above the cowshed.

Trudi and Toni soon found the nets, which were stored in the workshed. For the next quarter of an hour they hammered nails into the walls so that the netting could be fastened to them.

They stretched a double netting across the cowshed, about five feet from the ground and directly underneath the hole in the roof. If anyone fell, the netting would save him from injury.

Grandfather Hoffman patted Toni on the back. "If ever I say you are a stupid boy, as I have once or twice in the past, just remind me of these nets. It is a clever idea, Toni."

Toni got one of the smaller farm spades and was starting up the ladder again when Trudi stopped him with an urgent cry. "Wait a minute, Toni. If you do fall, and a lot of snow comes down, you might be buried again."

"I'll have to risk that," Toni said.

"But if you had a rope tied around your waist, and we had the free end," Trudi said, "we wouldn't have to dig you out, would we? We could just pull on the rope and . . ."

"Well, well, well," Grandfather said, and now the old chuckle was back in his voice. "You are as clever as Toni. It is a splendid idea. What is more, as well as having a rope around your waist, you could take a rope up and tie it round Mr. Asche. Yes, we'll do that."

Five minutes later Toni was again climbing, a rope round his waist and another in his left hand. His spade was tied to his right wrist by a piece of string.

When he reached the hole in the roof he discovered that the heat from the lamp he had left in the snow cavity was already melting the snow above it. Water was beginning to drip onto the top of the lamp. Each time a drop struck the hot metal lamp shield, it hissed and spluttered.

Down below, Trudi and Grandfather watched and waited anxiously. Trudi held the rope which went up to Toni's waist, and Grandfather held the other one which was to be fastened around Hans Asche's shoulders.

It took several minutes before Toni was able to get the rope around the limp airplane pilot. Finally, however, he managed to secure it.

"I'm going to start digging now," he called down. "So you had better stand clear. I can't see where I'm throwing the snow."

"All right," Grandfather shouted back, and drew Trudi with him to the doorway leading into the workroom. The first shovel of snow tumbled down, striking the pile already on the cowshed floor and scattering in a flashing spray of white crystals.

Trudi and Grandfather could hear Toni grunting each time he dug his spade into the snow. It was packed quite hard, for above it was a layer of snow almost thirty feet deep.

Thump . . . thump . . . thump . . . thump! The snow came down as regularly as the ticking of the big old clock, and Grandfather Hoffman shook his head, then called up, "Take your time, Toni. A few minutes won't make so much difference, and if you get too tired you could easily slip."

The sound of the spade ceased and Toni called down that he was going to rest. He was panting and had already begun to perspire. As he wiped the tiny beads of moisture from his forehead he suddenly realized that the man trapped in the snow was looking at him.

Hans Asche had begun to feel a little better. The hot coffee with the brandy had given him fresh strength. And his dead feeling of despair had started to lift as he watched Toni wielding the spade, gradually enlarging the opening in the snow. For the first time since he regained consciousness, Hans began to feel that there might be a chance for him.

He cleared his throat. "Are you Austrian or Italian?" He had forgotten where he had been when he had parachuted from his burning airplane.

"Austrian," Toni said, startled at hearing the man speak. "I . . . I thought you were unconscious again. Are you . . . hurt?"

"I think there is something wrong with my legs," Hans replied. "But if I can get out of here . . . the doctors will soon put that right, I'm sure. Will it be long before you dig me out?"

Toni hesitated. He did not know how to answer the man. Dare he tell him that the more snow he dug away from him, the greater was the risk of them both being thrown down to the floor of the cowshed below?

"I'd better get on with the job," was all Toni said.

Hans Asche lay and watched. It was a queer, frightening feeling, to be trapped in that tiny snow cave. The boy with the spade was only two feet from him, and behind the youngster was a simple oil lamp. In the close space its light seemed quite brilliant. Hans could see the sweat on Toni's face, and could hear him grunt each time he dug the spade into the snow.

Toni was cutting the snow from under Hans, and having to be careful that he did not strike the man he was trying to rescue. As he watched, Hans saw a fragment of snow fall from above the boy. In the lamplight it flashed for a second as if it was studded with diamonds. Then it dropped out of sight.

Hans looked up at the snow above Toni's head. It

had several cracks in it, and he could not keep his eyes off them. Were they growing larger? He closed his eyes for a moment, then looked again.

He was sure now that the cracks were widening. He passed the tip of his tongue over his dry lips. Should he warn the boy—tell him to get away before the snow fell?

Hans closed his eyes. He was frightened. He had been buried so long in the bitterly cold snow that the idea of being deserted, even by this boy, sent a shiver of dread through him. He watched Toni for another minute. The boy was making progress. Each time his spade came out, the snow was looser under Hans. He could breathe more easily. Perhaps the boy would rescue him after all.

Against his will he looked up above Toni's head again, and this time there could be no doubt—the cracks were growing wider all the time. It would not be long before the roof of snow fell in on them.

A tiny voice at the back of the German's mind reminded him, "If you warn the boy, he will go away and may not be able to come back. Don't say anything for another minute or so. He may still be able to free you before the snow caves in."

Hans looked again at Toni. The boy's face was flushed with the effort he was making. This digging was hard work, and he was gasping for breath. His chest was rising and falling as he struggled to free him.

"You are a coward, Hans," the trapped man told himself. "You cannot let this boy die just because of you. Tell him the danger. Tell him . . . NOW! Before it is too late."

He drew in a deep breath, then said, "Boy, I have forgotten your name . . . but you had better stop digging. Get off the ladder quickly. The snow above you is going to fall. It is cracked. Don't waste time looking up. Get away before it is—"

Hans never had a chance to finish his warning. Before Toni could move, the snow caved in. It rushed down like a gigantic waterfall, blotting out the light. One moment the snow was lit by a golden glow, the next all was black.

Down below Trudi and Grandfather gasped at the sudden torrent of snow which came pouring down. Masses of it struck the rope netting which they had stretched across the cowshed in case Toni fell. The netting did not break, but the strain was too much for the nails so recently hammered into the walls. Some were jerked out, while others were pulled straight, allowing the loops of the netting to slip off. The net was dragged to the ground and hidden under the rising pile of snow.

The mound was eight feet high, and covered the width of four cow stalls. Grandfather Hoffman and Trudi could only stand and stare. Where were Toni and the man he had gone up the ladder to rescue?

8 :: A GHOST IN THE CHIMNEY

:: "Pull on your rope!"

Grandfather Hoffman suddenly came to life and began heaving on his rope. Trudi pulled the rope she held, but as soon as it went taut she could do no more. The tautness told her, however, that the man who had been a prisoner in the snow above the roof was now down in the cowshed. When the snow fell, he had fallen with it.

"Give me a hand," Grandfather bellowed, already puffing as he hauled on the rope he had tied about his waist. In the light of the single lamp they pulled, and after only a few seconds Toni was hauled out of the heap of snow, waving and kicking.

The moment he was free the two turned to pull on the second rope, which Toni had fastened around the shoulders of the airman. After heaving desperately for a few moments they dragged him clear. Unlike Toni, Hans did not struggle—he was limp and seemed lifeless.

Trudi helped her brother to his feet, and he stared at her for a moment as if he did not know where he was. He wiped the snow from his face, tried to scoop some from under the collar of his shirt, and wriggled as the snow slipped down his back and began to melt.

"What happened?" he panted. "I was just beginning to get him free when something went wrong."

"Never mind that now," Grandfather Hoffman said, giving Toni a squeeze about the shoulders. "Are you hurt—I mean apart from bruises?"

"I . . . I don't think so. Everything started pouring down on me. I felt the ladder beginning to fall, and I think I threw myself backward. I got snow in my face, and then . . . I fell flat on my back in the snow."

"You have the lives of a cat," his grandfather said, wiping a bead of perspiration from his own forehead. "If you had fallen before the snow made a nice cushion for you, well . . ." He shrugged.

Trudi went into the house for a blanket and Grandfather told Toni to put his ear against the rescued man's chest to discover if his heart was still beating.

"You fell soft," the old man said. "He may not have been so fortunate."

"But he was, Grandfather," Toni protested as he knelt down. "He fell after me. I felt something heavy plump into the snow just by my side."

"I hope he isn't too far gone," was the sober reply. "Ssshhh! Here comes Trudi."

They moved the limp figure onto the blanket, and

then somehow struggled with him through the work-shed and into the house. They were all breathing hard when they finally laid their burden down in front of the big kitchen stove.

"Now . . . what do . . . we do?" Toni puffed. "Really he should be in a warm bed, shouldn't he?"

"If you can carry him upstairs, Toni, we'll put him to bed," Grandfather said, with a twinkle in his eyes. "I think we'd better try and make him comfortable down here. First we must get his clothes off."

"They're stiff, aren't they? Half frozen," Trudi said, feeling at the bottom of the trousers.

"What are the cows bawling about?" Grandfather suddenly asked. "They have plenty of hay."

"It's milking time," Trudi said. "We'd just begun milking when Toni remembered hearing the man's cry."

"Oh, yes. Well, suppose you start the milking again while Toni and I see what we can do for this poor chap."

Trudi went out to carry on with the milking, leaving Toni and her grandfather to do what they could for Hans Asche. Toni spent the next fifteen minutes trying to rub some life into him. He used a rough towel, and finally Hans began to murmur and groan.

Leaving Grandfather to try to get Hans to drink some hot coffee, Toni went upstairs for bedding. Like most Austrian farms, there were no blankets on the beds, but instead, huge feather-filled coverings which were not only soft but also very warm.

Two of these were laid on the floor to form a mattress, and a third they put over Hans. Toni looked at the mug of coffee standing nearby and was about to ask how much the airman had drunk, when Grandfather said, "I'm worried, Toni. He took a little, and he tried to thank me, but he needs more than warmth —he needs a doctor. I don't know what we can do for him. He has no strength, and his heartbeat doesn't sound very strong to me. Feel your chest, then feel his."

Toni put his hand inside his shirt and could feel the beating of his heart quite easily. But when he placed a hand over the German's heart, it seemed much slower, and at first Toni could not be sure he was feeling any heartbeat at all.

"Maybe the people from the village will get us out by morning," Toni said hopefully. "They must have got up here by now, don't you think?"

Grandfather scratched behind his ear again before replying soberly, "They may . ... they may; but if the snowslide was as big as I think, they may have had difficulty in getting here. There will be the risk of starting loose snow sliding again."

"You mean we may have to stay here longer than tomorrow?" Toni could not hide his dismay at the thought of being cooped up that much longer.

"People have been snowbound for a week," Grandfather pointed out. "Not that I think we'll be, but we might have to stay another twenty-four hours."

"Then what about him?" Toni pointed to Hans.

"We can't do anything now. It will be dark outside," his grandfather said. "But tomorrow, we'll go up to the attic. It may be possible to dig our own way out. Anyway, don't say anything to Trudi. No point in her worrying too."

Toni went to help with the milking, and afterward he and Trudi carried the milk upstairs and stood it near the window which they had managed to open earlier. The half-opened shutter allowed them to draw in snow which they heaped around the milk churns to keep them cool.

By the time everything was cleaned up, and more water had been given to the cows and Gretl, both children were tired. As they went down to the kitchen again they were greeted with a mouth-watering smell. Grandfather Hoffman had not been idle, for there was toasted cheese and sausage sizzling away in a big dish inside the oven.

After they had finished eating, they took their coffee cups and relaxed by the stove, which glowed pink with heat. The old grandfather clock in the hall struck ten.

Toni gasped. "Surely the clock must be wrong. It can't be so late. Why we . . ."

"That clock has not failed since I was a boy," Grandfather Hoffman assured him. "I used to say it was wrong when my mother told me it was time to go to bed; but it has always been right. It *is* ten." He took out his big silver pocket watch to show Toni and Trudi that it was indeed that hour.

"We *have* been busy, you know," he pointed out. "I feel as if I've done a week's work since the snow came down. But no matter—you two had better go to bed. I'll stay up with the pilot. In my time I've done all kinds of things, and I can surely be a nurse now."

"No, I'll stay with him," Trudi insisted. "Since I'm going to be a nurse when I grow up, I can practice now. I won't go to sleep," she added quickly when Grandfather seemed about to say No to her request.

The old man pondered for a moment. He was very tired, and he had a suspicion that if he did stay down here in the kitchen, where it was nice and warm, he might drop off to sleep quite quickly. He stood staring at the silent figure of Hans Asche for a few moments, then said:

"I'll tell you what we'll do—we'll share the night. Toni can stay up for the first three hours. Then he can wake you, Trudi, and I'll get up after you have done three hours. I always wake up early anyway, so it won't be any hardship if I get up at four o'clock."

For a moment it seemed as if Trudi would rebel at this idea, but Toni was already opening the door of the stove in order to stack it up with logs. Once the stove was filled, the draft could be shut down and the stove would purr away quietly until morning.

"Keep a good eye on him," Grandfather Hoffman said to Toni before following Trudi out of the kitchen. "If you think he seems worse, call me. Though I don't know what I could do if he became very ill. We'll just have to hope for the best. Perhaps a warm, quiet night will help him. Good night, Toni, and don't go to sleep."

"I won't," Toni promised, and went out into the hall. He stood at the door and watched his grandfather take a last look at the cattle and Gretl. A few of the cows were already asleep, others were contentedly chewing their cud. The pony was standing with her head drooping, and it was difficult to tell if she was asleep or awake.

When the bedroom doors had closed Toni went back to the kitchen, and for the first time since the airplane crashed, the house seemed at peace. With his shoes off, and wearing a pair of goatskin slippers his mother had made, Toni was just settling into the comfortable rocking chair when Fritzi, their cat, appeared. Where he had been during the excitement of the day Toni had no way of knowing, but the cat's black fur was plastered against his sides, making him look much thinner than usual.

Toni felt a pang of guilt when he realized that not once during the rescue of the animals from the cowshed, and then the rescue of the pilot, had he even thought of Fritzi. Everyone in the family took the old cat for granted. Just in time Toni stopped Fritzi from leaping up onto his knees. "No you don't, not when you are wet through," he murmured, and walked over to a cupboard where Mama kept old pieces of toweling.

Fritzi meowed his appreciation as Toni rubbed him dry. The cat had been dozing in the sun by the cowshed wall, as he did every day, when the snow came down. Afterward he had spent hours digging his way out to a drain hole which led into the workshed. Only a few minutes earlier he had finally managed to rescue himself and get back into the house.

Toni gave him a basin of milk, and when he had finished it, Fritzi leaped onto Toni's knee. It was very quiet. Toni had turned down the oil lamp, so there was only a subdued light in the room. The few sounds from upstairs had faded, suggesting that Trudi and Grandfather Hoffman were in their beds.

Ten minutes went by, then Toni sat upright. He was so comfortable in the chair that he had started to drop off to sleep. He only realized it when his head suddenly slipped off the side wing of the rocking chair, rousing him.

"Better sit straight up, or I'll be fast asleep in two

winks, won't I, Fritzi?" Fritzi didn't even meow. He was comfortable in Toni's lap and seemed to be sound asleep already. Then, from the far side of the room, came a sound so faint that Toni didn't hear it. Fritzi, however, lifted his ears, and his contented purring died away. One eye opened and he looked in the direction from which the sound came.

Field mice crept into the house every year when the first snow fell, and stayed until the spring sun had uncovered new grass in the pastures. During the daytime, the mice kept out of sight, but they ventured out at night when the house was quiet. They were after any tiny crumbs that Mama Hoffman might have missed when she swept with her old-fashioned broom.

Toni felt Fritzi stiffen, and turned to look in the same direction the cat was staring. A tiny field mouse came out into the lamplight, and behind it were two other mice. Fritzi remained absolutely still, his muscles tense, and Toni knew that if the mice came any nearer, the cat would jump one of them.

"Go home," Toni called, and as he spoke Fritzi leaped from his arms. The three little shapes vanished into the wall, and the cat slithered the last foot like an automobile that had suddenly been braked. He mewed his disappointment, for all three mice had escaped.

The incident helped Toni stay awake, but even so the three hours he was on watch seemed longer than

a whole night. The clock struck eleven, then ages passed before it struck the quarter hour.

Finally, however, it was one o'clock. Toni got up, stretched and yawned, and made a cup of coffee to take up to Trudi. She came down and settled in the kitchen armchair, quite determined to keep wide awake. But the room was so cozily warm, and Fritzi's purring so soothing, that without realizing it she drifted off to sleep before two o'clock struck.

Fritzi woke her just before the clock struck six by bouncing off her knee and screeching. What had alarmed the cat Trudi did not know, but his screech made her heart thump and her cheeks tingle with fear. She was even more startled when the clock in the hall began to strike the hour.

One swift glance at the cat told her something really was wrong. Fritzi was no coward, but now his back was arched and his fur was standing on end, just as it did when someone came to the farm with a strange dog. What was more, he was spitting in the direction of the stove.

He backed toward Trudi and rubbed himself against her legs as if wanting to be assured that everything would be all right. Trudi's heart was still beating loudly, but she could see nothing out of the ordinary, and the house was quiet. She shot a quick glance toward Hans Asche, who still lay as quiet and peaceful as when she had begun her night watch.

"Well, what is it, Fritzi?" she asked, kneeling down and stroking the cat. "Did you have a bad dream?"

Then she heard the sound which had frightened the cat. It came from the stove—a strange kind of roar. Trudi knew at once that it wasn't the moaning that they heard often enough when winter winds howled across the mountainside. Winds made queer sighing and groaning noises in the chimney pipe; but this was different. It was a frightening sound—half roar, half wail.

Fritzi was so startled he clawed his way up onto Trudi's shoulder and perched there, his eyes shining as green as the greenest emeralds. He arched his back again, and spat defiance at the stove.

The sound stopped as abruptly as it had begun, leaving the room somehow quieter than before. Trudi was conscious of her pounding heart; she clasped her hands because they were beginning to tremble.

To break the silence, she spoke to Fritzi. "You old silly," she whispered, "it's only the wind in the chimney pipe. You've heard it before." Yet the cat remained tense on her shoulder, and she could feel his claws through her dress.

She waited and waited for the sound to come again, but all remained quiet. Remembering she had heard the clock in the hall sound the hour, she tried to think how many times it had struck. She knew she should have awakened her grandfather at four. Feeling guilty for sleeping when she should have been keeping watch, she picked up the lamp and went out to check the time. It was just three minutes past six.

Trying to think of an excuse she could give to her grandfather, she hurried back to the kitchen. There she was greeted, not by the frightening roar she had heard earlier, but by a new, startling noise—the rattle of metal on metal. Trudi stood in the kitchen doorway and stared around. Her gaze rested first on Hans Asche, but he still lay exactly as he had throughout the night.

Rattle-rattle! There it was again! Trudi looked up, for the sound seemed to be coming from just under the ceiling—from the stovepipe! Something must be coming down the stovepipe, she guessed. Clutching the cat under her right arm, Trudi rushed from the room, shouting for Toni and her grandfather.

9 :: MESSAGES

:: The house suddenly came to life. The cows had been asleep, for they never awoke until the new day came or a light was brought to the cowshed. But Trudi's frightened yell brought them all to their feet instantly, and they began to bawl excitedly. Gretl, a nervous pony, was also startled, and she reared and tried to break her halter rope. Her hoofs slipped on the smooth wooden boards of the hall, and she went down with a thud which seemed to shake the house.

There were cries from upstairs. Neither Toni nor Grandfather had undressed before going to bed; they had merely taken off their shoes so they could be ready in a moment if anything went wrong.

Toni came galloping down the stairs two steps at a time, his face mirroring his fears for Trudi. Only able to hobble, Grandfather Hoffman was a very poor second.

As her brother jumped the last few stairs into

the hall, Trudi was suddenly ashamed at her panic-stricken yell, and without waiting for Toni to ask what was wrong, burst out with explanations. In a breathless rush, she told him how the cat had been frightened, and then about the rattling sound in the stovepipe.

"What time is it?" Grandfather asked. He had managed to get near enough to hear Trudi's tale, and since there was not sufficient light in the hall to show him the face of the big clock, he had no idea what hour it was.

"About ten minutes past six," Trudi said.

"But I thought you were going to wake me up at four," Grandfather said.

"What about the noise in the kitchen?" Trudi retorted. She did not want to have to explain now that she had fallen asleep.

Trudi and Grandfather followed Toni into the kitchen. With the door shut, reducing the noise from the cows, it was almost quiet in the big room.

"There was a clanking from the stovepipe," Trudi insisted, anxious to defend her screams. "I didn't yell out just for fun. I wouldn't do that. You know I wouldn't."

"Don't worry," Grandfather said. Turning to Toni, he suggested, "Open the stove door . . . and stand to one side. Something may have fallen down the stovepipe. You never know."

Toni got the metal hook with which they opened the fireplace door. Trudi and Grandfather stood several yards away, silent and expectant. Toni whipped the door open and stepped back.

Nothing happened. Nothing fell out. Nor was there any sound. Bending down, they could see the glowing heap of wood ashes. They began to glint brighter as air rushed in through the open door, fanning the dying fire to a greater heat.

"Well, there doesn't seem to be any . . . wait a minute." Toni was standing nearer the stove than the others, and he caught sight of something at the back of the fireplace, amid the remnants of the logs. "There is something there. Looks like an old tin can. Did you put a can in the fire last—"

"I never touched the fire," Trudi interrupted impatiently. "You were the last to stoke it, and the door hasn't been opened since."

"If you can get . . ." Grandfather Hoffman began, then stopped, for from the heart of the fire itself came a roar, almost like someone shouting down a narrow tunnel.

Now that she had her brother and her grandfather with her, Trudi was not so startled as before. "There you are. I told you I heard something strange. It even scared Fritzi, and he isn't easily frightened."

"Get the can out, Toni," Grandfather Hoffman ordered, frowning. "I may be wrong—I hope I'm not—

but I think someone may be shouting down the chimney. If the people from the village are here, then the tin can might contain a message. I have known that method to be used in avalanches before."

Toni had to make two attempts before he managed to grab the can with the long tongs they used for moving wood in the fire. He finally succeeded, but only because his grandfather had told him to wrap a wet towel around his hand and arm. The stove fire had burned low, but there was still a great deal of heat coming from it.

Trudi brought a bucket of water, and they splashed some onto the can, which had been burned blue by the heat. Their eyes shone with joy when they noticed that a piece of wire was fastened to the tin—a wire which extended up into the chimney.

Now there was no doubt at all. The rattling sound in the pipe had been made by the tin can as it was lowered down the chimney. There *were* rescuers in the snow above the house.

They had difficulty lifting the lid of the can, for the heat had stuck it tight. Only after he used a hammer to knock the can out of shape was Toni finally able to wrench off the lid. Disappointment awaited them. There had once been a piece of paper inside, but while the can was lying in the red-hot fire, the paper had become a fragile brown curl which crumbled into dust when Toni tried to pick it up.

"Don't worry," Grandfather Hoffman said. "If they can send a message down to us, it means the villagers know where we are. Get some paper, Trudi."

"But won't that burn too?" Toni asked.

"Not if we wet it well. Just write: *Grandfather, Toni, and Trudi all safe and well. House seems in no danger. Beware of the cowshed. The roof is falling in.* "I put that in, in case they try digging from the back," he explained.

Trudi was just finishing the message when Toni asked, "Shouldn't we say something about Mr. Asche? We'd better tell them he needs a doctor."

"A doctor?" Trudi's voice showed sudden alarm. "I thought he would be much better now. He seems to be sleeping."

"It is his breathing," Grandfather told her. "He does need a doctor. Ask if there is one with them, and explain the situation."

Trudi added a note about Mr. Asche, saying he seemed very ill. Then the paper was dipped in water. The ink blurred a little, which worried Trudi.

"They'll be able to read it," Grandfather Hoffman assured her. "Now, Toni, put it in the can and give a gentle tug on the wire. Don't jerk it, for it may not be very strong."

Toni tugged on the wire, and was delighted when, almost immediately, it tightened and the can was drawn up into the stove. All three of them watched anxiously as it was yanked through the red embers of the fire. Then it vanished up the chimney.

"Hadn't we better put the fire out?" Toni asked, and at a nod from his grandfather he began to draw the glowing wood embers out while Trudi damped them with water. The result was the same smell they had noticed when snow first came down the chimney; but this time they were happy. With the fire out, it would be easier to receive and send messages to the people up above.

A few minutes later there was again a rumbling sound from the fireplace. Someone was shouting down the chimney, but the words were so distorted by the pipe that it was impossible to understand a single syllable.

"Shout back, Toni," Grandfather Hoffman said, "then they'll understand that we can't talk to one another this way."

Though the red-hot ashes had now been drawn out of the fireplace, the heat was still great, and Toni had to mask his face with a wet towel before he could get near enough to shout into the chimney.

Five minutes later there was again a clatter and a metallic rattling from the chimney pipe, and this time Toni was ready with the tongs. With his arm again protected by a wet towel, he scooped the can from the bottom of the chimney, and waited while Grandfather opened it. This time the paper was not even browned by the heat.

Grandfather Hoffman took out his steel-rimmed spectacles and perched them on the end of his nose. Holding the paper near the lamp, he began to read:

We're so glad to know all three of you are safe and well. We got here just before sunset, but even with lights brought by an army helicopter we could not locate the house until an hour ago, when someone found the place where the heat from your chimney had melted a hole in the snow.

It's good to know Mr. Asche is with you. A big search has been going on for his plane, and no one knew where to look. Doctor Spiedal is here, so if you let us know what is the matter with Mr. Asche he may be able to advise you what to do. Everything is going to be all right, though the army people think it may take another 48 hours before we can dig you out. Your mother and father send their love.

Grandfather paused for a moment before adding, "And it is signed by the Mayor himself. You see how important we are."

Both nodded, but neither Trudi nor Toni was smiling. Forty-eight hours more was a long time to be imprisoned in the snow-covered house, and they looked anxiously at the silent Hans Asche.

"We'd better have a look at him," Grandfather said, breaking the silence. In an effort to cheer up his grandchildren he said, "The doctor will know what to do, once we tell him how Mr. Asche is."

There was little to see, however. The pilot simply

lay there, very still, very pale, and breathing heavily. After a few minutes they composed another note in which they tried to explain the condition of the patient—his heavy breathing, and their inability to awaken him.

The tin can was again sent up the chimney, and ten minutes later it came down with a message from Doctor Spiedal:

It seems to me as if the man might be suffering from pneumonia. We are going to try to dig a tunnel down to the attic window. If we succeed, we will try and get Mr. Asche out that way. In the meantime, keep him very warm. Don't try to give him anything to drink unless he really wakes up. If you can put hot bran poultices on his back and chest, so much the better. Don't worry. We will do our best to get to you quickly.

There were several sacks of bran in the workshed, for the cattle were fed on this food from time to time in the winter. It was made into a mash with hot water.

Neither Trudi nor Toni knew what a poultice was, for they had never been seriously ill. Grandfather Hoffman knew, though, and he chuckled as he poured a generous helping of bran into a big bowl. Toni had already put a pan of water on to boil, and using this, the old man mixed the bran and water into a stiff mixture, very much like the porridge they gave to the cattle.

"We put this on his chest," he explained when the bran had become really stiff.

"On his chest?" Trudi looked horrified. "But won't it scald him?"

"We'll wrap it inside a rag," Grandfather explained, spreading out a piece of cloth. "Then we'll tie it up into a bag. How the heat works I don't know, but it does help people with illnesses like pneumonia to breathe more easily. Mind you, we'll have to keep changing the poultice. As soon as one begins to cool, we'll need to put another hot one in its place."

All morning long Trudi saw to it that the bran bags were kept warm. She wiped Hans's forehead and lips with a cool, wet cloth, and watched eagerly for any sign of him wakening. No nurse could have been more devoted.

Since Trudi never left the kitchen for more than a minute, she was the one who received the bad news in the afternoon. She had just put on a fresh poultice, steaming hot, when the chimney pipe rattled again.

She shouted for her grandfather and Toni. They had been forced to relight the stove fire, for without it the house would very soon have grown extremely cold. Before lighting the fire, though, they had sent a message to tell those attempting to dig down to them that they were doing so. Thus any message now was bound to be an urgent one.

Toni grabbed a towel, soaked it in water, and

wrapped it about his hand and forearm. Then he picked up the fire tongs and opened the stove door. A wave of heat came out into the room. Toni, with the rag about his hand already beginning to steam in the heat, poked his tongs into the fire, and was lucky to grab the can at once.

The moment it was out of the fireplace, Toni dropped it with the tongs and dragged the smoking rag from his arm. Then he swung his arm around to try and cool it quickly.

Grandfather Hoffman poured water over the can and got the lid off; he took out the message, but did not read it aloud. The children became anxious.

"Something wrong?" they both asked together.

"Hm," Grandfather said, and pursed his lips for a moment.

Toni waited, but Trudi couldn't hold back. "Grandfather, never mind trying to think of a way to make the news sound good. There's something wrong, isn't there?"

For a moment the suggestion of a smile made the old man's lips twitch. "You are altogether too sharp for me, young lady. Yes, I might as well tell you at once, there is something wrong. The hole they were digging down to the attic window has collapsed. The sides fell in . . . and they don't think there is a chance of getting to us for some time. Perhaps not until to-morrow."

Trudi finally broke the silence that followed. "Hans isn't any better," she said soberly. "I think he is worse. Grandfather, *we've* got to do something."

Both children stared at their grandfather, and the old man automatically felt for his pipe. Slowly he stuffed tobacco into it and struck a match. But he was so worried he held it in his fingers until the flame burned down and scorched his thumb.

Neither youngster spoke. Their grandfather was thinking. He *always* knew what to do. Surely he would know what to do now, for a man's life was at stake. This time, however, Grandfather Hoffman only shook his head. "If they can't get in, how can *we* get out?" he finally said.

"You mean we've got to stand here and let Mr. Asche die?" Toni asked, horror in his voice. "Grandfather . . . you *must* think of something."

The old man continued to shake his head, and admitted sadly, "I just can't, Toni. There's nothing we can do. We are prisoners—and the snow is too deep and thick for us to break out."

10 :: BREAKTHROUGH

:: Trudi turned away so that the tears which had suddenly filled her eyes would not be seen. Toni had a lump in his throat. After working so hard to get Hans Asche out of the snow above the cowshed, it seemed unfair and unjust that he should now have to lie here, and perhaps die, when there was a doctor just above them. Toni gulped and walked out of the kitchen into the hall.

Five minutes later he bounded down the stairs, an empty bucket in his hands, his eyes wild with excitement. He rushed into the kitchen and Grandfather turned so quickly that he almost fell. Trudi was taking off a poultice that needed reheating and looked up, startled by her brother's sudden appearance.

"I've got an idea," Toni gasped. "I went up for a bucket of snow, and I was thinking so hard I didn't realize where I was until I found myself in the attic. I'd just gone on climbing stairs—"

"The idea!" Grandfather interrupted. "Out with it."

"We could dig our way out from the attic," Toni said, and paused, expecting Trudi and Grandfather to become as excited as he was.

Trudi looked anxiously at her grandfather, but the old man just stood and stared for a moment or so, then shook his head. "If the snow above us is so soft that it falls in on men digging down, how—"

"But you haven't heard my idea," Toni said impatiently.

"Well, go on and tell us what it is," Trudi snapped.

Toni glared at her for a moment, then said, "I got the idea from the boxes in the attic. Suppose we pushed one through the attic window—after digging some snow away on the outside first. The snow couldn't fall in then, could it? And there are eight boxes up there. Couldn't we use them to make a tunnel so the snow wouldn't cave in?"

Trudi's eyes narrowed. The boxes had been in the attic as long as she could remember. They were filled with all kinds of things which no one wanted, but which Mama Hoffman refused to throw away. All of them were almost a yard along each side, and a yard high.

"We'd have to knock the bottoms out," Toni said, his eyes gleaming with hope. "We could do it, Grandfather, I know we could."

The old man had doubts, but the strain of doing nothing while the sick man grew worse was telling on him. He decided it might be better to try Toni's scheme than just wait.

After sending a short note to their would-be rescuers to say they'd wait for better news, the three stoked up the stove, and went upstairs. They took two spades, a length of rope, and several lamps. Toni also remembered to bring along a hand axe for knocking out the bottoms of the boxes.

While Grandfather Hoffman removed the bottom from a box which Trudi had emptied, Toni opened the attic windows and tried to push out the shutters. But the snow piled up behind them resisted his efforts.

"I need the axe," Toni said. "I'll be as quick as I can."

"By the time we've finished," Grandfather said, forcing a smile, "there won't be much about this house your mama and papa will recognize—what with cows in the parlor and now these shutters. I think they'll forgive us, though."

His pretended cheerfulness helped both Trudi and Toni. There had been little enough to laugh about since they had become prisoners. Trudi smiled as she busily emptied a second box, and Toni attacked the shutters with fresh vigor.

Chips of wood flew in all directions, and finally the

smashed shutters were battered off their hinges and thrown to one side. The snow looked like a solid yellow wall in the light of the lamps.

Toni dug his spade into it, and soon there was a growing pile of snow on the attic floor. He carved out a passage a little more than a yard square, and when the roof of the snow passage showed signs of falling in, he pushed the first wooden box through the attic window, and into the hole in the snow.

More snow was dug out and passed back to the pile

on the floor. Toni was now lying half in the box as he
dug. Then the box was pushed farther out, until only
its end rested on the window ledge.

"Better tie a rope round your waist now," Grandfather ordered. "Then if the snow does collapse we'll
be able to drag you back into the attic."

Toni did not argue and Trudi said nothing, but in
the yellow light of the lamps both their faces looked
paler than usual. Toni would now have to lie flat in
the box in order to scoop out the snow ahead.

He did this until he had quite a cave in front of
him. Only then did he realize that it was not ahead
he wanted to go, but up—up where there was fresh
air and sunshine.

His tunnel was about six feet long now, but only
the first three feet were protected by the box. He
inched his way back along it, and finally stood in the
attic getting his breath.

"What will you do now?" Trudi asked.

"I'll have to dig . . . er . . . upward," Toni said,
wondering if his idea was quite as good as it had first
seemed.

"What if the snow falls in?" Trudi asked, and she
could not keep anxiety from her voice.

"You'll have to haul me back; but I don't think it
will." Toni tried to make his voice sound assured,
as if there'd be no such danger. "What do you think,
Grandfather?"

"If Mr. Asche wasn't so desperately ill I wouldn't let you do it," was the sober reply. "If my legs were all right I'd do it myself. Be careful, Toni."

"Yes, do be careful," Trudi urged, "and if it shows any signs of—"

"I'll tug on the rope right away," Toni broke in hurriedly. "Don't worry, Trudi; I'm not looking for trouble. The point is, they can't get to us; so we must get to them. I'm going to start now. I'll shovel the snow into the box part, and you scoop it out into the attic. Who is going to hold my rope?"

"I'll do that," Grandfather said, and under his breath he murmured, "God be with you, boy; God be with you."

Toni crawled through the box and into the tiny snow chamber beyond. Then he began to dig snow down from the roof. He was very cramped, and it was not easy to scoop the snow back to where his sister was waiting to shovel it out of the box.

At the end of ten minutes, however, Toni's tunnel went up almost five feet. He still had to crouch, but he was finding the work less difficult. The light from the lamps on the attic window ledge lit up the bottom of the shaft. His lower legs were lamplit, but above there was only reflected light from the snow.

Carefully he cut out more snow, lowered it to the end of the box, then tried to tip it as near his sister as possible. He could not see her at all.

Suddenly a mass of snow fell in. Toni shook his head to clear it from his face, and without thinking he lifted his hand to wipe his eyes. As a result the spade handle struck the snow roof above him.

Whoosh! It was as if he had accidentally opened the catch of a trap door. Snow fell like a thick blanket from above him. It filled the shaft to his knees, to his waist, then to his chest, and it was still falling.

"Grandfather!" he yelled. "Pull . . . pull!" He tried to sit down, for he would have to get in a crouching position before he could be hauled back into the box, and on into the attic again.

He felt the rope about his waist tighten. Grandfather Hoffman *and* Trudi were hauling on it with all their combined strength. But Toni could not sink down into a sitting position, for the snow was like a cushion. It was all about him, holding him upright, soft yet strong. Each time he pushed at the snow it gave, but more fell into the space he had made.

He lifted his hands to clear the snow from his face, and the moment he did so, he stopped struggling. Snow was up to his neck, and above him it sloped steeply upward on all sides. He was at the bottom of a deep hole in the snow, but *his head was in sunshine!*

What was more, he could hear voices calling, though he could see no one. The rope about his waist was hurting. His grandfather and Trudi, back in the attic, were pulling with the strength of desperation, trying to drag him back to safety.

Toni reached down, and getting his hands on the rope, he started to jerk it as a signal. It was then he heard a voice, a voice filled with amazement, asking what seemed a very funny question:

"Hey, there, are you Toni Hoffman?"

Toni looked up. Some five or six feet above him, and looking down the snow slope, was a man's face. He was wearing a soldier's cap, and must have been lying flat on the snow.

Toni grinned. He suddenly felt ridiculously happy. He was out; he was in the open air! He *had* found a way!

"Don't make any movement," the soldier ordered. "More snow might slide down on you. I'll get help."

Toni heard other voices, but saw no one for some minutes. The soldier had called the rest of the rescue party who were busy on another attempt to dig down to the house.

Soon a score of men were digging a wide trench at a gradual slope down to the spot where Toni was waiting to be rescued.

In the attic Grandfather Hoffman and Trudi were still struggling to haul Toni out. Trudi wanted to crawl into the tunnel in an effort to rescue her brother, but the old man would not let her. Snow had already half filled the box when the upward shaft collapsed.

"We can only try to get him back this way," Grandfather Hoffman panted. "Come on, get hold of the rope and we'll make a last . . ." There he stopped, for the rope, which had been hanging slackly in his grip as he waited for Trudi to grasp it, suddenly tightened.

There were one, two, three little jerks.

"What's the matter?" Trudi gasped when her grandfather showed no signs of wanting to begin pulling again.

"The rope jerked," the old man said softly. "Maybe . . . maybe something has happened that we didn't expect. Wait . . . I'm going to tug on it," and he pulled gently, once, twice, three times.

Trudi's face was as white as the flour her mother used for baking bread; her eyes were wide with fear. Then she felt the rope jerk in her grasp, once, twice, three times. She stood motionless, overcome not with horror but with sudden joy.

"Jerk again," she commanded, and waited for the reply. It came—three slow and deliberate jerks. Then they knew. Toni was still alive; even though his upward shaft had collapsed, he had not been buried.

Twenty minutes later there was a slow pull on the rope. Grandfather and Trudi allowed it to slide through their hands—then the pull ceased.

"Should we pull now?" Trudi asked, and when her grandfather nodded, she began to haul on the rope.

Within a minute she had brought in a tin can tied to the rope. Grandfather Hoffman snatched off the

lid, held the message near the lamp, then let out a
long sigh. Without a word he passed it to Trudi. She
read it, read it again, then blinked as tears of relief
and joy filled her eyes.

The note, from her mother, read:

*Toni is safe with us, and it will not be long before
you are dug out. The soldiers and men from the village are just making sure the snow will not fall in
again, then they will come for you. Love from us all,
especially from Papa and Mama.*

Forty minutes later the soldiers, aided by men from
the villages in the long valley, had dug a deep sloping
channel down to the attic. Grandfather Hoffman and

Trudi were helped out of the house. They were met with cheers and more cheers as they came up the snow slope.

The sun was shining from a cloudless sky, and the air smelled sweet as if spring were only a few days away. Trudi found herself in her mother's arms, and Papa clasped Grandfather Hoffman.

Toni, with a sandwich of bread and sausage in his hand, stood and watched. He had already been hugged and kissed by his mother, whose cheeks were wet with tears.

Several soldiers, carrying blankets and a stretcher, wriggled their way back into the attic for Hans Asche. There were villagers standing everywhere, and an army helicopter had brought up a camp kitchen, from which blue woodsmoke was curling up into the sky.

The chattering of the onlookers died away when the soldiers struggled out of the attic window with Hans on their stretcher. Doctor Spiedal spent a minute or so with him, then the stretcher was carried across to the helicopter. Before climbing aboard, the doctor took a moment to reassure the Hoffmans that Hans's life could still be saved.

The idling helicopter engine burst into a roar and the big rotor blades swung round quicker and quicker. Four soldiers crawled across the soft snow to free the big skis on which the helicopter had landed. They heaved and struggled for a minute or so; then the grip of the snow broke and the helicopter leaped into the air.

Very quickly it disappeared, rushing Hans Asche off to the nearest hospital. When the clacking sound had died to a murmur, Toni mentioned the cattle, and Gretl the pony.

"You are not going back in that house for all the cattle in the valley," his mother said firmly. But when the head of the rescue party assured her the men would dig a way down to the front door within forty-eight hours, Mrs. Hoffman finally agreed to let her two children return.

Grandfather Hoffman would have gone back, too, but Papa would not listen to such a thing. "They are my cows," he said. "And anyway, I want to keep an eye on Trudi and Toni. There is a nice warm place for you in the village, and you can go down in a sledge with Mama. You have earned a rest, Father. Now you can leave everything else to me and the children."

So, as the sky was beginning to darken over the snow-covered peaks, Trudi and Toni, with their father, went back into the house, using the attic window again. Grandfather grumbled, but he had a twinkle in his eyes as he climbed into the sledge and was made comfortable. There were other old men in the village, and it would be pleasant to sit by a big stove and tell the story of how he and his grandchildren had been held prisoners by the snow, and how they had to bring the cattle and a pony into the house.

In the house the cows were protesting. They knew it was long past milking-time, and they wanted more hay and water. But the house also rang with happy songs as Trudi and Toni, and their father, set to work. The snow would soon be gone, and life would go on as it always had. The danger was over.